Best

Carolyn R.

PRAISE

Russell

"In this YA dystopian thriller, a teenage girl fighting against a fascist government learns an astonishing truth that changes everything.

After environmental disaster and ensuing wars, the future … seems grim for most. Seventeen-year-old Somerset Whitman is more fortunate … her family are clerics, and for generations they've lived in a huge 'Tempedral,' where, Somerset says, 'It's our job to … brainwash Seekers into requesting Reverie'—an event that no one returns from. Secretly, Somerset works with a resistance cell.

… With intelligence and energy … Russell creates a believably paranoid atmosphere and shows how propaganda and advertising contribute to propping up fascist governments. However, the book never feels didactic, thanks to Somerset's naturalistic narration and well-rounded characterization. An intriguing and thoughtful adventure."

Kirkus Reviews

"*In the Fullness of Time* is what the best YA dystopian novel strives to be; a prism through which present-day issues can be explored that leaves readers—young and old—satisfied, entertained, and yearning for more. Set in a future world destroyed by chemical alterations to the biosphere, seventeen-year-old Somerset Whitman struggles to make sense of a theocratic government that values its own comfort over the lives of its citizens. Yearning to reconcile what she sees and hears on the crowded streets to the official 'States' position, she enters the resistance. There, she learns truths that force her to question family and loyalties. Russell's simple prose allows Somerset to tell you her story through the unblinking eye of a youth emerging into adulthood."

Connie Johnson Hambley, author of *The Jessica Trilogy*

"The ruined landscapes and corrupt inner sanctums in Carolyn R. Russell's *In the Fullness of Time* are depicted with a cinematic flair that pairs beautifully with her gift for suspenseful story-telling. A riveting adventure that rockets toward an ending I'm still thinking about. Highly recommended."

STEVE BLACKWOOD, ACTOR, DIRECTOR, SCREENWRITER, AND AUTHOR OF *THE BLACKWOOD SESSIONS*

"*In the Fullness of Time*'s dystopian world evokes an evil worthy of its fiery protagonist's rebellion. In Somerset Whitman we have a heroine for the ages: irreverent, compassionate, and unstoppable. *In the Fullness of Time* is chock-full of indelible characters, and the fast pace of the action makes for a page-turningly addictive read."

ELIZABETH LORAYNE, AUTHOR OF THE *PIRATESS TILLY* SERIES AND *THE HISTORICAL HEROINES BOOK: PIONEERING WOMEN IN SCIENCE*

ABOUT THE AUTHOR

Carolyn R. Russell was born in Massachusetts and moved back with her family to Boston's North Shore after many years of writing, teaching, and travel. A movie buff since childhood, she has taught college film aesthetics and film history in addition to other subjects. *In the Fullness of Time*, her third book, began life as a screenplay. Carolyn was surprised to learn it had other plans for itself.

Please find more at www.CarolynRRussell.com

IN THE FULLNESS OF TIME

CAROLYN R. RUSSELL

Vine Leaves Press
Melbourne, Vic, Australia

Print Edition
ISBN: 978-1-925965-28-5
Published by Vine Leaves Press 2020
Melbourne, Victoria, Australia

Cover design by Jessica Bell
Interior design by Amie McCracken

 A catalogue record for this book is available from the National Library of Australia

For Morton H. Rubin

Easy peasey lemon squeezy
Make my burden light and breezy.
We go in, we don't come out.
Everybody! Twist and shout!
Easy peasey lemon squeezy
Make my burden light and breezy!
Go!

—States Children's Game

CHAPTER ONE

I am so late. The crowd carries me backward almost as often as it lets me move forward, and today I don't have the time to surf its filthy waves. My loathsome cleric's tunic hangs loose and open because I didn't do up the front before leaving for my teaching duties; the civilian cottons underneath my uniform are partly visible. Not that anyone in this suffering, sweaty mass would care, but I want to be more presentable by the time the teachers at Randall States School see me. The last thing I need is to draw attention to myself, especially negative attention. Not with what I'm up to in my spare time.

The rhythm of chaos has a beat all its own, and I wait for a break. Eventually someone will stumble or fall, and, in the confusion, I'll be able to grab enough space to push my kinky dark curls underneath my headdress as per regulations. Then it happens. I hear the cry of a child, and I turn to see a small girl bending over to grab her foot. It must have really hurt for her to do that. She's violating the first rule of modern pedestrian travel: keep moving. This girl seems to be out on her own. If she falls, she'll be trampled. I leap backward, shoving several people aside. Their curses ring in my ears as I lunge for the girl, and I manage to catch her before she hits the hard-packed earth. No one attacks us, though, and I'm momentarily grateful for the status my rigid gray uniform confers. The girl puts her arms around my neck and holds tight.

"Don't let go," I say, already in motion again. "What's your name?"

At first, I'm not sure the girl will be able to say a word. She looks around five. Her little face is bright red with emotion and, I assume, daily prolonged exposure to deadly sunlight. Her tiny hand maneuvers one of her tangled white-blonde braids into her mouth, and I'm impressed with the strength of her one-handed grip.

"Monica," she says.

"Monkey? Did you say your name was Monkey?"

"No," she says. "Monica ..."

"Your parents named you Monkey?" I say. "That's a weird name."

"No, not Monkey," giggles this kid. "My name is MOOOONICA."

"Okay, Monkey. Let's see if we can pick up some speed here. My name is Somerset. I'm on my way to Randall, where I volunteer. When we get there, we'll find your mom or dad. Hold on very tightly with *two* hands. Which I bet you can do, right Miss Monkey?"

"OOH OOH HAH HAH!" Monica screeches in a fine imitation of the beast in question. There haven't been real monkeys around for a very long time, a clue that the girl's parents are at least well-off enough to have shown her holo-films or old-timey flatbooks. I figure I'll be able to track them down at school using its Hydracomputer. When I find them, I'm hoping to be able to control my temper. Which I've never been good at. But anyone who could lose track of a child deserves its shock and awe.

The Randall School is the same as most States buildings except for its size. The institution sees fit to educate only the children of States officials and clerics, so it's relatively small. Like all the other official structures in the States, its façade is elaborately decorated with images I've secretly researched: cruciforms, Stars of David, crescent moons, yin-yang, Mickey Mouse ears, Nike swooshes, McDonald's double arches, and other, less easily identifiable emblems. They all compete for attention, even as they merge into a meaning-less jumble of symbols and ideas. Underneath, of course, all construction in the States is the same, built entirely of recycled materials from the Lost Ages. As we slip through a side entrance reserved for teachers and staff, Monica reaches out to touch the door's unadorned upper back surface, a bumpy expanse of broken china. "Careful," I say, grabbing her hand. "It's sharp in some places."

I put the girl down on the floor, out of reach of the colorful shards. Aside from a slight favoring of her left foot, Monica seems fine now that she's indoors. I quickly guide her down the hall toward my classroom, hoping that my kids are still inside and moderately quiet. I'm only here to help, of course. My eighteenth birthday is months away. Mrs. Wagner is the States-appointed Kindergarten teacher. But Mrs. Wagner is old enough, as the saying goes, to recall iced tea. When I come, she disappears to wherever she goes to take her breaks and, I suspect, down whatever substance she uses to survive her daily ordeal, life.

Fourteen scrubbed little faces greet me and Monica. The

room is filled with barely suppressed excitement, and I remember. This morning will be devoted to another school pageant event, and all my charges are dressed for the occasion. The only thing I hate more than my own uniform is having to see my six-year-olds in their miniature versions, unwittingly advertising the power of the States and its monstrous control over all our lives.

Mrs. Wagner comes back and gives me a grateful nod, and I quickly organize the kids into two lines and usher them toward the back of the building. I scoop Monica up into my arms; the school medico will be in the auditorium with everyone else, and he can check the girl's foot. Then after the performance, I can Hydra her parents.

The auditorium is already full when we arrive. I settle my class on the floor at the lip of the stage, in front of the seated older students and teachers. I scan the room for Dr. Szabo, but there's no time; the play is about to start.

"How about we watch a show before we find your family, Monkey?"

She beams at me and settles on my lap as the lights dim and then go dark. A single spotlight illuminates a high schooler holding a script. Colored lights slowly come up behind him, turning the stage an acid green and purple. As the boy begins to speak, young dancers pour onto the stage.

"Part Two," the boy intones solemnly. "During what are now known as the Lost Ages, the Earth heats up, and the climate changes create new opportunities for various species to thrive. Humans are tortured by the disease-spreading mosquito, the only creature on our planet believed to be superfluous to its ecosystem, unnecessary to its food chain. Malaria, dengue fever, Zika virus, and nuevoencephalitis are just a few of the illnesses that devastate communities and cause lethal suffering. Eventually, the death toll reaches millions."

As the narrator speaks, the performers behind him interpret his words. Kids in black costumes with insect-like wings "attack" citizen dancers, who fall dramatically to the stage floor.

The narrator pauses. He looks at the audience and gestures, his fingers mimicking tears falling from his eyes. His face is blank of emotion. So creepy. I check on Monica, who is motionless in my lap, her head against my shoulder. She seems fine.

"Scientists develop a way to combat this most dangerous foe of Mankind. They create a genetically modified mosquito. When it mates with natural mosquitoes, the offspring die. Soon, there are no more mosquitoes." The dancers behind the narrator skip happily about the stage, twirling in circles and clapping.

"The plan works very well," the boy says. "However, once the mosquitoes and their diseases are gone, scientists discover that they were wrong. The species they destroyed did play a vital role in the ecosystem. Mosquitoes kept the human population on Earth in check. Without them, the population explodes. There isn't enough food or water or energy for everyone."

Kids zoom onto the stage now, and the space becomes too crowded for movement. They pretend to fight with one another in small clusters.

Monica turns in my lap and looks up into my face; for the first time, this tiny girl is crying.

"It's okay," I say, hugging her. "It's just a show. It'll end soon."

The narrator continues.

"People organize themselves into separate groups based on religion, ethnicity, and politics to survive the massive scale overcrowding and limited resources. Wars begin. They are very terrible and impact all aspects of life on Planet Earth."

The lights in the auditorium go off. When they blink on again, the dancers on stage are holding hands and smiling.

"But that was long ago, before the Reorganization. Now we all believe in ourselves, and there is no more fighting. Faith and science have converged. We are united under our Faction, the States," says the boy.

Two youngsters dance onto the stage hoisting a banner with the distinctive B-bar logo emblazoned upon it, and the words "Nutribrix. For Life."

The boy looks down at his script.

"We are all now well-fed and taken care of by the States food initiative, Nutribrix. Under Grayson Taft, no one goes hungry."

A young girl in the audience groans audibly. I look behind me to see the girl's teacher, Mrs. Collins, cover her student's mouth. She glances around before we make eye contact. She looks away.

The dancers end their performance with a balletic finale. "Best of all," the young narrator says, "we have been offered Reverie, The Gift to us all. One day, when the time is right, each of us will find joy in the convergence of all that is good. This, we are promised. In the fullness of time."

The performers bow. As the audience bursts into applause, I hide my face in my headdress, pretending to straighten it. It would take a split siren to interpret my reaction to this putrid propaganda otherwise. I hold Monica tight, and wonder again where she comes from.

It seems to take forever for us all to file out of the auditorium. When I get back to the classroom with my students, we find Mrs. Wagner dozing by what passes for a window; the children of the well-born are sheltered from any views that might disturb them by semi-transparent, beautifully hand-decorated sheets of Plexie. The old woman wakes up slowly and, it seems to me, regretfully. I explain Monica's predicament, and offer to find Dr. Szabo and do the Hydrasearch.

"By all means," says Mrs. Wagner. "You know I can never figure out how *best* to make that blasted thing work. I'll keep an eye on things here."

I thank her. I'm loving her careful word choice; it's commonly understood that Mrs. Wagner is not to be trusted with a pair of scissors, let alone a Hydracomputer.

"Let's go, Monkey!" I kind of sing, and I'm rewarded by a small smile.

The girl self-consciously smooths back her pale hair and puts her hand in mine. Those braids, I think, were made by someone who loves this child. It's now my job to locate them.

"Who are your people, honey? What are their names?"

Monica's face crumples, and I'm afraid she's going to cry again.

"That's okay, Monkey. We'll find them. Right now, let's get you to the doctor, okay?"

We find Dr. Szabo in the library, thumbing through a catalogue of scientific holofilms. He looks up and takes off his glasses.

"Doctor, this is Monkey," I say.

"I'm Monica," she says. "There's no such thing as monkeys!"

"No," says Dr. Szabo, "but there used to be. Did you know that?"

"They lived in trees and ate bananas," says Monica.

"More or less," says Dr. Szabo. "Actually, more, then less, then none at all. How can I help you two?"

I describe Monica's fall, and her slight favoring of one foot afterward. Monica, for her part, points at the afflicted ankle. This kid is adorable.

"Does it hurt you now, little one?" asks Dr. Szabo, removing her shoe.

"No, not so much now," says Monica. "Somerset saved me."

"Why the tears, then?" asks the doctor, gently tracing the girl's cheekbone with his thumb.

"We just saw Part Two of this year's pageant," I tell him.

"Ah," Dr. Szabo says. He mutters under his breath. "Highly inappropriate for such young children."

The man startles with a sharp intake of breath. He looks around the room, and then at me. I smile at him with what I hope reads as sympathy, and he seems to relax.

"Let's have a look at that foot."

I sit with Monica while the doctor does a quick exam.

"You're a healthy Monkey," he says to Monica. "And you, Miss Whitman," he says to me, "are a good citizen."

"Excellent news, aye Monkey? Let's go find where you belong," I say. "Thank you, Doctor."

As we leave, I turn my head to see Dr. Szabo at the sight-less library window, his head resting against the Plexie. He looks up at me and raises his hand in a weary goodbye.

There's a long line at the school's Hydra. When I finally get my turn, Monica looks very tired, and probably, I think, more than a little hungry; my kindergarteners will have finished lunch by now. So, the first thing I do with the Hydra is call my mother. We've been having a tough time together lately, but I know I can always count on her in a crisis. Especially when she finds out that this one involves a child in need.

When my mother arrives, I'm surprised. She's pulled her clerical hood as closely as she can around her face and used its transparent veil to cover her mouth and nose. She's getting soft, I can't help but think. Or maybe the stench of the city is getting worse and I haven't noticed. In any case, Meredith Whitman has broken her own record for foot-speed. From the stricken look on her face, I can guess why. I missed curfew twice last week. Plus, there's been some other stuff; I'm not sure how much she knows, or what she's been able to guess. She probably assumes I'm in trouble again.

"Well, hello young ladies," my mother says softly. She reaches beneath her tunic to a hand-sewn compartment in the lining. I have a miniature e-tazyr in mine; it's small but produces a current strong enough to incapacitate three large men. My mother retrieves a Nutribrix bar from hers and hands it to Monica, who tears open the wrapping and shoves the bar into her mouth in one quick motion. I wonder how long it's been since her last meal, and I feel terrible that I didn't feed her immediately. What was I thinking?

I meet my mother's eyes and no words are needed. Another victim of the States' "austerity measures." Slow starvation for those unlucky enough to be low born. But I watch as she takes in the child's braids and clothing and grasps the paradox. This child comes from circumstances that should have put her well beyond most of the crueler realities of life in the States. And yet. She is clearly very hungry and looks like she's been out among the sun-bleached multitudes without a bath for a very long while. My mother arches an eyebrow at me, and I shake my head. I know as much as she does.

She gives me a quick kiss on the cheek and takes me aside. "No idea who she is or where she's from?"

"Not yet. But I'll find out. You know I'm pretty good with a Hydra."

My mother smiles. "Yup, I know," she says.

Recently there had somehow been a little issue with extra water allocations directed to the city's poorest citizens. In a moment of weakness, I amazed my family by being able to explain exactly how the "mistake" might have been accomplished from a compromised Hydra portal.

"Can you take her home, Mom?" I ask. "Her name is Monica. She's not saying much right now, but maybe later. Can we just take care of her for a bit? Until we find her people?"

"Of course, honey," she says, walking toward the girl. "I was about to suggest that. What do you say, Monica? Will you come home with me to Somerset's house?"

"Somerset calls me Monkey," says the child. "'Cos I can hold on tight."

"Monkey it is," says my mother.

I hug Monica, now officially Monkey, and wave. "I'll be home a little late tonight," I say. "Don't you and Dad wait up. I'll make the curfew siren." I leave quickly, before my mother can muster a response that might ruin our fragile truce.

***

After school I head to my part-time internship via the tunnels that connect all the States Government Center buildings. I feel a sharp and guilty pleasure in the temper-ature-controlled air and relative spaciousness; I can swing my feet a bit without touching anybody else. It's just the deuce, and I try to allow myself to enjoy it. The job itself is more boring than I imagined it would be, but it allows me into a world most citizens are barred from. My uncle, Criss, set it up. He's a sweetie, my dad's half-brother. Also Head Cleric, very upper echelon. So, he gets what he wants. And what he wants is for me to understand the inner workings of a system I despise. It's my job to do designated tasks and sit in on most of Grayson Taft's meetings; that's who I'm assigned to. He's our States Director, the ruling tyrant of our Faction. I learned recently that our area used to be known as New England. As far as I know, Taft answers to no one, but does consult with the directors of other Factions from time to time. I imagine that evil must be coordinated to achieve maximum impact.

I enter Taft's fancy conference room and take the empty chair next to his. I'm in time to catch my second show of the day. After a short introduction I don't even listen to, the room darkens and a wall-sized holofilm lights up. Two magnificent humans lift their arms over their heads, their perfectly sculpted bodies clearly visible beneath their gauzy white robes. Hands clasped, they rise, ascending into a vibrantly hued sky. The pair gaze at each other in ecstasy and begin to soar through a visually stunning fantasy world in a state of perfect bliss. A logo blinks on, two interlocking W's and a question mark. Words appear below the logo: *REVERIE. Why Wait?* The holofilm ends. I want to vomit.

All eyes in the large airy conference room turn toward Taft. Other government officials, their aides, and assorted guests wait for his verdict. Taft takes his time, smoothing back a stray lock of unreliably dark hair, and sighs. He turns to his assistant, Nan Wilder, and raises his eyebrows. Nan shrugs in response.

Taft speaks directly to a meek-looking man at the table. "Flying, Bailey, really?"

Dale Bailey answers nervously. "The focus group results are irrefutable. The imaging diagnostics would blow your mind! This spot initiated stratospheric synaptic responses. Everyone wants to fly. Must be at the core of our collective unconscious."

Taft turns to Nan. "What the hell. Did he just say."

"It's tested well," says Nan. "People will like it."

Taft regards Bailey again and waits before speaking. His eyes bore into Bailey's, who seems not to know where to look; he decides that the gold epaulets on Taft's ridiculously ornate uniform are a safe place to settle his gaze. Like countless tyrants before him, Taft has a flair for the dramatic. Finally, he answers. "It's fine. It'll do. Use it for all the new billboards."

Appearing relieved, Bailey sits back in his chair, and the meeting continues. "How are the new mobile Kiosks coming along?" asks Taft.

A woman I don't know speaks up. "We hope to have all of them delivered by Decemberday. But our numbers are off. The opposition seems to be making some small inroads, especially in the West End. But we'll catch up again, it's only a matter of time."

Taft grunts. "Isn't everything?" The room stills. This kind of remark is often a prelude to a full-blown tantrum.

"When is Decemberday?" asks Nan quickly.

"We'll be told soon," says Taft. "Comments? We need to bolster participation as quickly as possible."

"My feeling is that we need to do a better low-level campaign," says the woman. "Boots-on-the-ground citizens convincing folks that it's the right thing to do … for themselves and for the States."

I watch as Taft and Nan exchange an ambiguous look. "Yes, well …" Taft mutters. "We shall, of course," he booms, "persevere." He hisses to his aide under his breath. "Can't stand these earnest true believer types. Lose her. Get someone more …."

"Practical?" whispers Nan.

"Realistic," says her boss.

WHAP! An explosion at the window behind Taft's head startles only me. I'm still not used to this, even though I've learned it's not an uncommon event: a rock secured inside stained Nutribrix wrappers and heaved at a Government Center window. It bounces harmlessly off the military-grade glass and falls to the ground below, where I imagine it will be crushed under the feet of the relentlessly miserable.

The meeting goes on and on. After a couple of sirens, Taft begins to wrap things up. For the first time he makes direct eye contact with me, handing me his tablet and asking that I file it. He tells me to give my uncle his best, which earns me a grimace from several of my fellow bureaucrats. I don't blame them. Not for that, anyhow.

I am dismissed not much later. The aroma hits me hard as I exit the building, but it's one I'm used to. Human body fluids of all kinds form a top note. Undertones of rancid cooking oil and beer. And fire, always the acrid smell of fire.

The trick is to focus on the footwork required to achieve speed and anonymity. I'm almost home when I ease around a corner and see it. A pop-up market. It's crazy busy now, but in a few hours, it'll be gone. The reason these shops come and go so fast is that they are less actual markets than tables of goods under new management. As in stolen.

I love these places. My dad and I used to haunt them when I was a kid. I don't think it ever occurred to him that they were illicit; he has always assumed that everyone is like him—honest. It was so much fun to look at the crazy mish-mash of items for sale or barter, and it was like watching a holofilm to see the different vendors selling their stuff. They told jokes and stories, and some even sang songs about who they were and what they had on offer. Every-body wore the same bland, beige sun cloaks, but these were the most colorful people I'd ever seen. My dad and I have spent countless hours in their company. Best of all were the antique flatbooks. They changed my life. Later I realized how ironic it was that my dad encouraged my obsession with them; the seeds of a rebellion against nearly everything he believed in hid within their covers.

CHAPTER TWO

Monkey holds tight to my hand. Despite every effort, no trace of the tiny girl's family can be found. We've grown to love her; she's one of us now. Her presence at my side feels like the only thing anchoring me to this moment. We pass the huge Kiosk-holographic billboard: the ubiquitous two interlocking W's and a question mark. Its headline reads "Reverie – Our Gift to You." I want to throw a rock through it. I want to scream. I want to be anywhere but here. Though everyone assembled waits for us, I walk as slowly as I can down the decorated path. The courtyard is near empty and bizarrely serene, walled off from the rest of public space. I guess it's a practical effort on the States' part to calm those about to witness or undergo Reverie.

I've done everything in my power to stop this day from happening. Hours upon hours, months upon months of argument, persuasion, threats, and tears. I had every hope I'd be able to change a course set in motion before I was born, even though I was dealing with the only person on Earth more stubborn than I am. And then, just like that, it was decided. He decided. And we both ran out of time.

Monkey looks up at me.

"You're sad?"

"Very, very sad," I say.

"But looking happy?" Monkey asks.

"It's important to smile," I say. "People are watching. Cameras."

Monkey nods, and I wonder at how easily this girl can adjust to her circumstances. What must she have endured to earn this adaptability? I'm coping not at all. As I join my family, I look at my older brother, Matthew. Like me, my mother, and Uncle Criss, he wears a festive version of the formal clerical uniform; golden threads shoot through the habit's traditional gray material. They all wear their finery with an ecstatic energy that I can't begin to mimic. True believers, I think, as they begin to sing. My best friend, Serena, standing slightly apart, begins to play her violin, a piece she's composed herself. She catches my eye, and I have to look away; her face is a study in pain and sympathy, and it nearly undoes me. We all clasp hands as we stop before the Kiosk and wait. It is unendurable.

The symbols and designs on the façade of the building begin to swim. I'm hoping my tears will be mistaken for those of joy. My mother shoots me a worried look, and I begin to clap to the rhythm of the Song of Reverie. Satisfied, my mother looks away.

The door of the Kiosk opens, and my dad is there.

Dad!

Saul Whitman raises his arms, and we all rush forward into them. I'm breaking apart. I can't do this. My dad steps back and delivers the Benediction. He waves, and strides back into the Kiosk. I don't know I'm falling until my knees hit the dirt.

***

I don't remember much from afterward. Stiff, shiny fabrics against my skin, strong arms around my shoulders, the feel of my mother's soft hand against my forehead, smoothing back my hair. I wake up and wonder how many sirens I've missed. I can hear the celebration below, in the reception area of our Tempedral.

Yeah, I'm *that* Whitman, one of the Tempedral Whitmans. Generations of my family have lived here in this huge place while others go homeless. It's our job to take care of the ornate building and brainwash Seekers into requesting Reverie.

There's a knock on the door and before I can manage a sound, there is a beige-colored blur and then Serena is next to me on my bed. She gives me a quick hug and settles in, her head on my shoulder. Something bangs up against my knees and a surge of thankfulness makes my heart beat faster; it's her violin. Serena looks at me and I nod, and she removes her instrument from its case.

Serena plays the violin like she's discovered another means of being human in this world. She writes her own stuff, music that feels less like composition than the transliteration of raw emotion. Tonight, I can tell she's improvising, and I relax into the hypnotic strains of a melody that's barely a melody; it sounds like wind. Serena closes her eyes. Mine remain open and glued to the silver teardrop charm attached to the top clasp of her violin case. My dad gave it to Serena when we were little.

After she finishes, we're quiet for a while.

"I wish I could say something to make us both feel better," I say eventually.

"That's kind of funny," says Serena. "You're the one usually so good with words."

"Yeah, well, words have their limitations," I manage. "I couldn't talk Dad out of revving."

We both pretty much lose it then.

***

When I wake up, Serena is gone, and it's morning. Time to leave my room, make an appearance, and deal with the fact that today will be an ordinary day as far as my family is concerned. Except we'll have to greet the visiting well-wishers congratulating us on Dad's Reverie, and I'll have to pretend to be properly joyous; only our private family area is unsurveilled.

I find everyone in the kitchen, and my mother gives me a hug when I come in. I can't help it; I can feel myself tense in her arms.

"We have coffee today. If you hurry, you'll have time for a cup before your school shift," says my mother.

"Coffee coffee? Or some noxious crap Taft says is coffee?"

Matthew looks all upset, and I feel bad. Matthew is pure. Monkey looks from my mother to me and waits. But my mother lets it go.

"Please remember to wear your veils today. The air's up past ten," she says.

"It's never past five in the Government Center buildings. Big surprise," I say.

"Somers," says my mother, "I'm very much afraid that at some point, you'll go too far. Your father and I always encouraged your singular brand of ...."

"Don't you even talk about Dad!" I yell. I'm beyond

caring. "You just let him walk into that horrible place and DIE! You never even tried to talk him out of it!"

I slam my way through the Tempedral to my bedroom, as loudly as I can; I know I'm being childish, but I can't stop myself. I want my family to know how I'm feeling, suffer for it, and worry about me. My room is its usual crazy mess, but I know where everything is. I have a collection of old-timey artifacts that take up most of an ancient wooden crate that lives under my bed, and I pull it out now. Beneath the plastic fragments, metallic pieces, glass bits, and paper pictures of foods that no longer exist, I find it.

I know from my reading that Styrofoam was outlawed over a century ago. That's why my dad and I were so amazed to find a decent-sized piece of it a few years ago at a pop-up. Nobody else seemed interested in it, and we bought it for very little. Dad carved a little animal figure out of the stuff, a four-legged indeterminate creature we named Pal. Pal keeps me company now as I give over to my tears.

***

It takes a few days before I leave home again. My mother makes it easy for me to grieve privately for a while, and I'm glad of it. I've written nearly every night of my life for years, and I try to focus everything I'm feeling onto the page. The only one I can bear to spend time with is Monkey. She brings me comfort, food, and tepid water, and she keeps me caught up on her life, which consists mostly of States schooling. We talk about what she's learning, and I try as gently as possible to caution her against the crud they're shoveling. I also try, as gently as I can, to find out about her life before she came to live with us. Monkey passively resists these fishing expeditions, going quiet and blank-faced. What horrors has she endured? I can't bear where my fearful imagination takes me.

***

My first day back on the grid, I don't dress in uniform. I don't have to because I've decided to ditch today's regularly scheduled program and be where I'm most needed. I grab my satchel on my way out.

I pull my suncap as low as possible as I move through City Center. I have to admit, it's not just to protect my eyes and face; the reality of how most people in the States live is almost more than I can take right now. I have extra Nutribrix in my pockets, and I give them away until they're gone. My family is lucky enough not to be totally dependent upon B-bars, but any other food might attract attention. The still-rising heat and the smell of unwashed bodies are nearly unendurable, and for a shameful moment, I wish I was at Randall with my students.

My first stop: Liza's Laundro. It used to be a place where people gathered to wash clothes. I know from the antique flatbooks I've managed to read that hot and cold water were available for a small amount of currency that nearly everybody could afford. Cheap cold water! I can't imagine it. Now this place serves as a sort of magnet for the kinds of gambling games I've been warned against since I was in diapers.

I slink around the groups of players and head to one of the rusted, wrecked appliances lined up against the wall. I reach inside the second to last one on the left and retrieve my signal, a red-colored chip. I pocket it and leave; no one bothers me. I move on.

I'm hot and filthy when I arrive at a hard-packed dirt lot filled with what used to be cars. Like pretty much everything else in the States, they've been hacked. "Repurposed," Uncle Criss would say. Some mostly intact ones are being used for storage, straggly-looking guards playing dice on their roofs. Others have people sleeping in them. One ancient truck hosts a cooking area on its flatbed; sun-cloaked citizens form loose waiting lines for whatever's on offer today.

I carefully pick my way toward the only red car I can see, throw my chip through the bashed-in front window, and squirm into what's left of the back seat. Serena's already there and hugs me, her silky auburn hair ticking my chin. I lean behind her to reach Stone and slap him on the back.

"Hey, Stone. You feeling better?" I ask.

"Yeah, sure," he says. "Takes more than a bad batch of 'Brix to get me down. Though it may have been the rotgut I drank with it that did the trick. Last time I throw someone a party, aye?"

"No good deed goes unpunished," I say.

"Right?" he says.

Serena starts to say something but this guy I've never seen before interrupts her, slamming his way into the car's ragged front seat and twisting around to look at us. The first thing I notice is he's, well, strange-looking. Not in a bad way. Like he's from a pirate holofilm from forever ago. He's maybe a year or two older than me.

"Who the hell are you?" I blurt.

"I was just going to tell you," says Serena. "Umm. Yeah. So, Riley's been picked up. She'll be in re-ed for a while. So, Jake here is gonna take over as cell head."

Oh, Riley!

This Jake person smiles at me.

"We're still on," says Serena. "Stone and me, we're the muscle this time. You guys do the thing. Not a lotta time here. Let's go."

"All in, baby," says Stone.

He and Serena exit the car and hurry off. Jake and I lock eyes for a moment before we get out. I'm not really the trusting type. And yet here I go, ready to leave with this stranger.

I secure my bag over my shoulder and I'm moving; I'm pleased to note that I've left him, literally, in the dust. He catches up, and we both weave in and out of the sweltering crowd separately, tracing a complicated path through the city. Still, we keep track of each other. We lose each other only once, when a FireSquad vehicle races by, horns blazing; the street-swarm is briefly united by its wish to survive what is often a lethal encounter between these States trucks and pedestrians. The States wants to save infrastructure, not people, and cares nothing for lives lost during the process. We foot travelers scramble to remain vertical as we dodge the truck, and even the most damaged among us try to flatten themselves against shelter. When the FireSquadders drive past us safely, Jake and I find each other. This time, he stays beside me.

"You know Serena a long time?" he asks.

"She's my best friend," I tell him. "Stone is a close friend, too."

"Stone, I get. But could you translate what Serena said? Muscle? The thing?"

"Our cell's been tight for a while now … I guess we use shorthand a lot. You'll get used to it, if you last." I guess I'm being harsh, but I'm thinking about Riley and the fact that she's now going through the horrors of re-ed; it's a risk we all run. I hope she makes it out still Riley-as-we-know-her. But I can't afford to dwell on that now.

"So?" he says.

"So, we're basically the distraction. Serena, Stone, and some others'll do the heavy lifting. Literally. We're after the B-bars and water tanks. You and I are going to put on these uniforms and ruffle some feathers." I reach into my bag and throw a clutch of fabric at him.

Jake catches the stuff. "Then what?"

"What do you think?" I snap. "How long you been doing this?" Ugh. I'm hoping I don't have to babysit the newbie all morning.

"I'm new as cell *head*. Just wanted to make sure I haven't missed any of your secret codes. These clothes won't be enough to get us inside. Got any eyeballs in that bag of yours?"

"Possibly," I say. "But we don't need to worry about the retscans because we're not entering the building. We're going to be between the warehouse and the truck yard."

"And our diversion?" Jake asks.

"Riley and I usually wing it. Like, a lover's quarrel or some such crap."

"Sure." Jake looks at me. "This could be interesting."

We change our clothes behind a blasted shed; modesty is one of the first things that goes when you're trained to operate within a cell, but we courteously avert our eyes. When we arrive on the edge of the warehouse property, we linger amongst the ever-present swarm of citizens milling about and wait for our opening. Right on schedule, uniformed men and women spill out of the warehouse's back doors, talking and roughhousing on the way to their trucks. Jake and I slip unnoticed into their midst. Then Jake yells at me.

"You wretched bitch! Why didn't you tell me?"

Wow. I didn't expect he'd jump right in so fast. But I laugh. A shrieky, kind of crazy laugh.

"I did tell you, you bloody moron! It's not my fault if you were too busy drinking yourself blind to listen!"

The gathering crowd likes this and starts to clap.

"Well if you weren't always so busy hauling your skinny carcass through every market in town looking for flatbooks, you could at least pretend we're in a marriage!" Jake yells.

I'm having fun now. "Worst mistake of my life! Just goes to show you, a pretty face doesn't guarantee a wretched thing south of the border! Or a surplus of anything resembling brain cells!"

The assembled throng cheers and hoots. Jake charges me and uses his body to back me up against a wall. He tries to kiss me, and I slap him hard across the face. Just then, the food and water truck engines roar to life; Stone, Serena, and the others furiously drive them off the lot. The States drivers run after them, shouting, and everybody turns their attention to this new entertainment. Jake and I make our exit, unnoticed.

We find a place where we can strip off our fake uniforms and change.

"Just the deuce," says Jake.

"How'd you know about the flatbooks?" I ask.

"A lucky guess. Got a question for you. How does a bloody Temprat learn to talk like that? Aren't you all bred from birth to roll holy?"

"Nature versus nurture. Are we born as we live or live as we are born?" I say.

"See," says Jake. "That's how I knew you read flatbooks."

He does this jaunty salute and takes off. I head in the opposite direction.

***

I get back to home sweet Tempedral and nearly topple Matthew over as I race past him to change my clothes. I've dodged school (maybe Mrs. Wagner won't report it?), but I can still make it to the Government Center on time if I rush.

"Somers!" yells my brother. "Why am *I* doing this?" he says, holding up a wet rag. He's doing my job, one of many I've ignored, cleaning the intricate carvings of the huge Great Hall. It's meant to impress people with the authority of the States and the clerics who do its dirty work. "Have you done any chores at all? Don't tell me you've even lifted a finger!"

I don't slow down. "You want me to show you exactly which finger I lifted, Matthew?"

I turn my head to see his reaction and feel bad; the poor boy is blushing to the roots of his hair. Like I said, Matthew is pure. Like our dad. Like our dad was.

***

When I arrive at Taft's office, he's not there. I sit down at his desk, and toy with the idea of trying to access his Hydra. Before I can decide if it's worth the risk, I hear voices coming from the office next door. It's Taft and Nan Wilder. Their connecting door remains slightly open, and I can hear every word.

Taft says, "Nan, you look exhausted. Why don't you rev next month and take your quivering piously pointy nose with you? Though, surely, it would be a pity not to pass those genes on."

Um ... What?!

"I take it you're not volunteering for the job," says Wilder.

"I might, if I wanted to risk spawning your unholy devil child," snarls Taft.

"Big talker," says Wilder.

"It might be worth it. Just to see if you actually bend anywhere. Alas, my heart belongs to another."

"To say they have my sympathy doesn't begin to cover it," says Wilder.

Okay. Not what I expected from these two. Not even remotely. I'm waiting for more sparkling repartee, but I hear Nan's heels click across the floor and then a thud. I risk a quick peek through the door crack and see that she's thrown a pile of HydraTablets down on her desk.

"The latest fodder for States History Week," says Wilder. "Watching this stuff ... We thought we were so smart. Ever shake your faith in science?"

I'm surprised Nan is giving him an opening like this. She of all people knows how much he loves to pontificate given any chance.

Taft goes into insufferable lecture mode. "In any age, the point is never to know absolute truth. It's to be amongst those who have access to truth-as-we-know-it-now. Or, truth-as-we-want-others-to-know-it. Of course, eventually, a new truth comes along, and we skitter like demented squirrels toward that new nut. But the nuts are more or less interchangeable. You see that, right? Hence our obscene goulash of Church and State."

"Lord help us all," says Wilder.

Taft snaps, "Out. Before I report that."

"It's my office," murmurs Wilder.

Before Taft can respond, somebody enters the room and leaves quickly. I hear the ripping sounds of a States-sealed courier folder being opened. And then Taft uses curse words even I have never heard.

"What is it?" Wilder asks.

He cusses like a madman again, and she pretty much runs out of her office. Here's the thing. She stops for a second in the hallway, glances into Taft's office, and looks straight at me. Her eyes widen, then she keeps on going.

CHAPTER THREE

It's a Freeday, and Serena, Jake, Monkey, and I sit on the dusty ground sweating, our backs up against a crumbling city wall. It's pockmarked with bullet holes, dents, and other artifacts of the war years. I'm doing my best to entertain Monkey, having told my mother that I was taking her out for a quick trip to the indoor "playground" available to clerical families. It's not that great; a big room with a soft-covered floor and a few toys, but it's better than where I've actually taken her. This place is a scrap of hell itself, and I'm really annoyed that Stone is late by at least two sirens. We've had a bunch of actions since Jake joined our cell, and Stone appears later and later for each one. I pull off Monkey's suncap to place my hand on her hot little forehead and smooth her hair back. Her curls are so different from mine: shiny, smooth, and practically translucent while my own are kinky, tight, and the darkest black. She puts her hand in mine, and I relish the contrast here, also. Hers is tiny, pale, and chubby, mine larger, dark, and bony. Stone emerges from the ubiquitous foot-traveling throngs, loping slowly across the ruined earth.

"Don't even go into it, Stone. Just sit down so we can

start," says Serena, and I'm glad. I'm in no mood for one of his colorful explanations.

"Please, let's hurry," I say. "We're expected at home."

Stone sits, and Jake begins drawing a diagram in the dirt. I give a rock to Monkey, and she starts drawing, too.

"Ante up," says Jake. "Great action the other night. The 'Brix went to the West End. Water went south. There's a lotta happy folks out there now. This next one is gonna be even bigger."

He goes on for a while. I confess, I'm not really paying as much attention as I should. I'm focused on two things: getting Monkey home before the sun and the air make her ill, and my plans for the evening. It's been planned for a long time, and I've got that nervous excited buzz that carries me through most of my extra-legal actions.

On the way home, Monkey asks me about my friends. "You have fun drawing?" she asks.

"Yes," I say, happy that I can answer her without lying.

"They're nice," says Monkey. "What game are you playing with them?"

"A dangerous one," I say, and she laughs.

When we get to the Tempedral, I catch up on some chores and look for Matthew. We're on the outs, but I also really miss him. I find him in the library, arranging the Reverential Articles of Faith in a fancy commemorative frame. I know what this means. He's been counseling a Seeker, and they've decided to rev. My heart starts to thunder in my chest. Matthew looks at me and stops what he's doing. He puts his arm around my shoulders and leads me to an alcove where we sit.

"What can I do, Somers?"

"Nobody can do anything to bring Dad back."

"Have you ever thought of doing an Experience?" he asks. It might help you to understand that we'll all be together again …"

"In the fullness of time," we both say simultaneously. Except I can hear the bitterness in my voice. He sounds like he always does, sweet and earnest.

"I'll think about it," I say to make him happy. He beams at me, and I feel bad for deceiving him. I have no intention of following through. Then it hits me. Maybe it would be useful to know what happens. Maybe it would help me understand why so many people choose to voluntarily end their lives and rev after an Experience, which is a sort of preview of Reverie. "I'll think about it," I say again, and this time I mean it.

Upstairs in the privacy of my room, I rest a little and go over my notes. I make some last adjustments to my writing and stuff my Plexie wolf mask under my shirt. As always on these kinds of excursions, I'm wearing civilian clothes that will afford me a lot of coverage for the sake of anonymity, and I steel myself for the ordeal ahead; it's very steamy tonight, even more so than usual.

When I get to the Government Center's gates, I take my position. We protesters loosely arrange ourselves in what's supposed to be a random spattering divided among the street mobs. A tall figure puts on their mask and raises a flag on a stick: the ubiquitous two interlocking W's with a red line drawn through them. Pretty basic, but it does the trick. Those of us there for the action follow suit, covering our faces with our Plexie wolf masks. We begin to read aloud simultaneously. Each mask contains a built-in amplifier, but it's a big space and I read my poem with as much volume as I can muster.

"Come home. All is forgiven.

Thus spake the souls of the newly shriven, consequence of a ruse:

The dead speak live,

Their songs extruded through our blood-soaked tithe.

And yet, in the fullness of time, may we all waken and arise!

In the fullness of time."

I feel a hand on my shoulder, and I freeze. This is it, the moment I've dreaded since joining my cell. I'm done for. Before I can begin to imagine the suffering my arrest and re-ed will cause my family and the damage it may do to the clerical caste I've grown up with, a voice I recognize as Jake's whispers in my ear.

"Take off your mask and come with me."

As he guides me out of the crowd, soldiers move in. One of them shoots his weapon into the air, and the noise is deafening. Everybody scatters, protesters and ordinary citizens alike. Jake keeps his hand on my arm as we twist and weave our way through the panic. It's both annoying and comforting. When we get clear of the commotion, he stops.

"One Trick Pony Café, don't make me wait," he says, and is gone.

On my way to the Pony, I stop to buy a disposable veil from one of the street vendors. It's embarrassing, but I'm practically gagging; I need another layer. The café is deep in the heart of the city, where the air, the heat, and the smell compete for which is worst. The cheap veil makes the trip more bearable. I move as fast as I can, taking a few shortcuts that I'm betting Jake won't know about yet. I arrive first and slam myself into a grimy booth a split siren before he spots me and heads over.

"You made me wait," I say.

He sits down opposite me. By now, I know him well enough to notice he's a bit off.

"You okay?" I ask.

"Compared to what?" he says. "My head aches."

"Poor baby. You want to curl up right here on the table and take a nap?"

Jake flashes me a sad smile before continuing. "I think it's the tear gas. I ran into it on the way here."

"Wow," I say lightly. "Escalation."

"Don't laugh," he says. "They actually killed three people. I overheard one of the medics. Probably a combination of the gas and the usual fun pollutants …"

I'm shocked into a rare state of wordlessness. I stare at Jake, and he grimaces.

"Taft's going off the deep end. We all need to be more careful."

I think back to what I overheard in his office. Taft is already crazy. Taft getting crazier is a scary proposition.

"This was in public?" I ask. "He's not even bothering to fake playing nice anymore?"

"That's what's so wretched. What makes him think he doesn't need to? Listen, change of plan. Our action is off for this week; I'll send word soon. I gotta go."

He gets up. I can guess where he's going.

"How much adrenaline do you need, Jake? How much can anyone stand?"

"It's not just the rush. It's the games themselves."

He slides back into the booth and this time we're shoulder to shoulder. His silky brown hair is pulled back into a ponytail, and I'm reminded of my first impression of him. Yup, I think, all he needs is an eyepatch and a parrot on his shoulder.

"The cutthroat competition, it's primitive. Calculating the numbers and cataloguing the endless ways people give themselves away. And how the cards take you to a different place, away from this steaming hellhole. Sweet Janus, we all need something. I'm late."

He slaps me on the back and leaves without a backward glance. I find I can't take my eyes off him until he's out of sight.

***

I'm worried I've missed curfew; the heart of the city is notorious for malfunctioning sirens. Sometimes it's sabotage. Most often it's that someone has figured out a way around the death grip the States has on the energy grid and siphoned off some lightning for themselves.

As I get closer to our Tempedral, I notice something weird. There are at least twice as many people as usual waiting at the front gates, which means there must already be an enormous number of folks seeking counseling in the Great Hall. I think back to the conversation I overheard in Taft's office. Wretched hell. That holofilmic billboard must have really done the trick.

I sneak in using a back entrance my dad showed me years ago. It looks as though a sharp bramble thicket makes the back of the Tempedral inaccessible, but there's actually a narrow path cut into it. It leads to a door, nearly invisible, but if you know right where to press, it springs open and inward to a space below the first floor in a rotted part of the cellar. Inside, I breathe in the earthy smells of dirt, stone, and damp coolness, lingering for a tiny bit to catch my breath.

Upstairs I'm able to blend in with the citizens in our crowded hall. Luckily, I have time to reach my room and change into my clerical uniform before I see my mother. Her face lights up.

"Somers! There you are. Can you please help Matthew with intake? All these Seekers at once!"

"Where's Monkey?" I ask. My mother gives me a sharp look, and I realize I've somehow blundered. Oops.

"She told me she had a reading lesson with you in your room. This was a while ago. Find her, put her to bed, and then help Matthew. Please."

I scamper to do her bidding.

I find Monkey curled up in a corner of my bed asleep. That I missed the fact that she was in my room with me while I changed clothes scares me; like Jake, I'm off my game. Monkey looks so peaceful I don't have the heart to wake her. I cover her with my thin, mesh bed topper and do some quick writing before I leave to find Matthew. Inspiration waits for no one, my dad used to say.

After processing the crush of Seekers and giving them appointments for Experience sessions, Matthew and I have a chance to talk. First, I give him the good news.

"I'm going to do an Experience," I tell him. Boy, does this make him happy. He hugs me hard and starts to fuss.

"I think it will be a turning point for you, Somers! And for our family. You'll see why Dad knew when it was the right time for him, and why he chose The Gift! Maybe it'll all make sense to you in a way it hasn't before …"

This bit surprises me. Before I can wonder what he means, he angles his head toward the Tempedral hall ceiling, at the cameras. With a shock, I realize he's covering for me, giving me what amounts to a recorded get-out-of-jail card for whatever States attention he thinks I may have triggered. Maybe at Dad's Reverie? Or after? All of that is still mostly a blur. I feel a surge of love for my big brother, whose protective instincts must surely clash with his most deeply held clerical beliefs.

"I think you may be right," I say. "One thing, though. Do you mind if I do my Experience with Uncle Criss's help, at his retreat? I'd like to do it more privately than here or at another Tempedral. Do you mind?"

"I don't, of course not," says Matthew.

If he's disappointed, he doesn't show it. In fact, he wishes me a good night, and goes to make the arrangements with Uncle Criss.

Now that I've committed to the thing, it starts to sink in, what I've done. Because the truth is, I have no idea what exactly to expect, or how I might react. So much effort goes into convincing citizens to do it. What if I'm changed by the Experience in ways I can't even imagine? I'm a little freaked.

No. I'm wretched scared.

CHAPTER FOUR

As a bona fide Seeker, I'll get some time off from school and my internship to get the full benefit of an Experience, which is fine with me. It's increasingly tough to be with my students, small hostages to whatever blather the States puts at the top of their agenda during any particular week. Plus, my work at the Government Center has lately been confined to the ultra-mundane. Even more so than usual. Only my powerful Uncle Criss could swing getting me a job so spectacularly superfluous. I can't imagine why my internship is important to him.

I take Monkey to Randall on the way to my uncle's retreat. I have to admit, she's adorable in her tiny school uniform, which somehow makes me madder than if it were hideous. I wear my festive cleric's habit, which I'll never wear again without recalling the worst day of my life. We're in an official car, which we try not to use too often; this morning, my mother insisted. Monkey and I look out the window, a transparent window, not Plexie. The landscape teems with citizens on foot, on scooters, in carts, and on bikes. Holo billboards flicker. A fire flares on the horizon. Monkey wants to get a better look at it, but I stop her from opening the window; too dangerous. To distract her, I point out the space and luxury of the inside of our car and tell her how lucky we are not to be out in the chaos.

"Why are we lucky, and not them?" she asks.

"That's a very important question," I say. "What do you think?"

"I think it's what you whisper about with Serena in your room sometimes."

This child misses nothing.

***

Our Tempedral is one of the most celebrated in the States and is large enough that its operation and maintenance keep our family very busy. It's nothing compared to Uncle Criss's retreat. It's less a house than a decorated fortress. It even has the kinds of turrets I've seen in flatbooks, and glossy floors made of real stone. As Head Cleric, he works with the Government, but mostly from here lately; his health hasn't been great. I find him waiting for me, resting in an armchair in front of a roaring bank of computers; half the States' limited energy must be diverted here.

I adjust the pillows behind him, and he pats my arm.

"How's everything going, little temprat?" he asks.

"Ha!" I laugh. "What does that make you?"

"I shudder to think," says the elegant old gentleman.

"I'm fine," I tell him. "No need to worry about me."

"I don't worry about you. You have your mother's strength and your father's vision."

"And you've never doubted this vision you share … shared with my dad? Ever?"

"I made a choice years ago," he says. "I still believe it was a good one, the right one. But I'd be a fool, or a monster, if I didn't sometimes entertain what used to be called 'dark nights of the soul.'"

He pauses and coughs, and I bring him some water. I'm thinking about what he's just told me; I'm sort of surprised by its lack of States-approved lingo.

"Ready, sweetheart?"

I'm not sure, and I tell him so. I've calmed down a bit since making the decision to do an Experience, but I'm still unnerved by the whole idea of it.

"I promise that no harm will come to you. Let us begin."

My uncle stands up, and I see how much frailer he's become since I last saw him; I make a promise to myself that I'll visit more often. He leads me down a low-lit gilded corridor toward elaborately wrought double doors. They open electronically, and we enter the Sanctuary.

The room is alive. Holographic images flow through and around us, and I feel a curiously weightless sensation. I'm untethered to gravity, floating in endless shades of blue. Gradually I am able to bring the space into focus. My life surrounds me. I stare at my mother as a young woman, holding baby Somerset in her arms. My father reaches out and catches toddler Somerset as she takes a first stumbling step. Matthew and I harmonize with Serena as she plays her violin. Me, in the Great Hall late at night reading flatbook poetry. Monkey, laughing so hard she spits 'Brix into my face and we both crack up. There's more. I can't take it all in.

"Wow." I say. "I wasn't prepared for this."

"I know it can be overwhelming. It's a tribute to Reverie's promise. Past, present, and future converging forever."

"And what if I loathed the color blue?"

"Then it wouldn't be your Reverie," says my uncle. "Would you like to begin?"

I nod, and Uncle Criss directs me to a beautifully embellished reclining chair. A bag of liquid attached to a tall pole stands next to it. My uncle rings a bell, and a cleric appears—someone I don't know—and does something with a clear, thin tube so that I'm attached to the pole, too. The last thing I hear is my uncle. "In the fullness of time," he says.

***

I'm drowsy when I sit up again. But in a good way, like when it's Decemberday, and your stomach is full. I stretch, and I'm dizzy, so I just sit, waiting for my head to clear. I touch the skin on the back of my neck, and it's sore; the brand's shallow grooves resist my fingertips.

A cleric enters the room, a different one from before. He asks me how I'm feeling and gives me a bowl of some mushy stuff to eat. It doesn't look like much, but it tastes really good. The cleric asks me to stay in the chair for a while longer, until I feel stronger. Then, he says, I can meet my uncle in his study.

When I feel steady, I make my way out of the Sanctuary. When I reach my uncle's study, I'm surprised to find him gone. I find a note with my name on it on his desk and grab it; in scrawled handwriting, he apologizes for an emergency that's taken him elsewhere. There's also a holofilm disk on his desk, half covered by a pile of HydraTablets, that's marked with a label: SERENA/CONCERTO. I grab that too and put it in my bag. I know my Uncle Criss won't mind; I'll tell him about borrowing it later. Monkey is in and out of here all the time; she can return the disk the next time she visits.

It's recommended that Seekers relax for a few days at home directly after an Experience, but I have other plans; Serena and I are scheduled to meet at the Pony. When I get there, she's waiting inside the door. She drags me to a booth.

"Bloody temprat!" she yells, hugging me. "It took so long! You've had me wretched worried. I thought you decided to rev or whatever!"

"I'll say goodbye before I go. You know that."

"Don't even joke," she says.

I laugh. "What have you been up to?" I ask.

"I want to hear about your Experience," says my best friend. She's blushing beneath her sunburn. Hmmmm.

"Spill."

"Stone," she says.

"Stone," I repeat.

"I know, don't say it. But desperate times call for desperate measures."

"You know I love Stone," I say. "But boyfriend material he's not."

"I'm not after a relationship. I just need a little fun now and then ..."

Stone would not be even close to my idea of fun, but if she's good, I'm good.

"Listen," she says, "before you tell me about today. I hate to ask, but do you have any 'Brix on you? I gave mine to my sister and her baby."

She's so embarrassed it kills me. And I hate myself for being so caught up in my own world that I forget what most citizens endure every day of their lives. I reach into my pocket for the stash I usually reserve for street kids, and hand them over. I have three, and as Serena takes them from me, I can tell she's trying not to rush.

"Let me see the thing," she says, her mouth full.

I turn my head and lift the back of my clerical headdress to show her the brand. I haven't yet seen it myself, but I know what she'll find: two interlocking W's with a question mark. Proof that I've done an Experience, and a barrier to ever doing it again.

"Yours is daintier than Stone's," says Serena.

"Stone did an Experience?" I stammer. Stone is more radical than I am. I can't imagine him even inside a Tempedral.

"Yeah. He said it was a good time," grins Serena.

Okay. That sounds like Stone.

I'm not sure what to say next, but I do my best to convey the feeling of an Experience. It was as if a door opened in my mind and suddenly I was part of each particle of substance in the world. I was lying in a chair in a room, but I was also everywhere else. I felt like me, but not-me. And I felt blissful, but also kind of distant, like I was observing my own emotions from far away. And wherever I was, I didn't want to come back.

Serena nods. "That's why it's a one-time thing. I heard it could be addictive. Can't have the Tempedrals clogged up with bloody thrill-seekers."

Thrill-*seekers*. She cracks me up. "Exactly," I say.

Serena has to leave at the next siren to start work; she's a server here at the Pony. A split siren later, I head out too. It's time I get home. As I reach the ramshackle entryway of the café, I catch a glimpse of Jake darting through the crowd outside. I don't know why I do this next thing. I just do it. I take off my uniform top layer and throw it to Serena, now behind the counter taking an order. She looks puzzled, but waves to me. I follow him in my civilian cottons, keeping my head low.

He's carrying something, snaking his way through the darkening city. I track him easily to a neighborhood I don't think I've ever been in before. I hear babies crying inside cardboard and metal shacks, people yelling and singing, kids playing. Along the fringes of the crowded dirt road are men and women lying on the ground or propped up against crumbling fences; citizens step over them as best they can. Jake is some ways ahead of me, but I manage to close enough space between us to see him meet a young guy, maybe my age or so.

"You got some?" says Jake.

"Yeah," the guy says. "I told you I could."

"How old?" asks Jake.

"Two minutes."

"Yeah, right, from where?" says Jake.

"Wretched hell," says the guy. "You don't want it, I'm gone. Already wasted half a minute."

"Like you'd know," says Jake.

The guy looks around and carefully pulls what seems to be an ancient wristwatch out of his pocket. Sweet Janus! I've only read about these things in flatbooks. Jake stares at it. Then he hands the guy a bag. The teen looks inside before he hands a package to Jake and takes off. Jake leaves at nearly a run. I follow him carefully, grateful for the cover provided by the congested foot traffic. A couple of streets away, Jake finds a small empty space up against a brick wall. I watch as he leans against it and opens his purchase. Something wrapped in foil. Jake raises his head and places the wrapping and its contents over his face. Eyes closed, he sways slightly and groans. I leave quick as I can.

My face feels like it's burning with a feeling I can't recognize or name. I begin my crawl home through the city on automatic pilot, slipping through the fissures and momentary ruptures of the writing crowd, the stream of my own thoughts foreign to me.

***

"You're not as stealthy as you think."

Jake is somehow right behind me, his body close to mine.

"I'm sorry," I say. I'm not sure why.

He slips his hand gently underneath the curls that tumble down my back. Tracing the new mark on the back of my neck with his fingertips, he sighs.

"To be fair, I didn't see you until you were leaving. So, you're moderately stealthy."

"I didn't …" I begin.

"It's okay," says Jake. "I've got a present for you."

He dangles something in front of my face, but I can't see what it is in the dark. Then I feel an exquisitely cold sensation; Jake is bathing my Experience branding with a piece of ice. He puts his other hand ever so lightly on my hip. The cube melts slowly into cool droplets that trail down my spine. Everybody and everything recede; it's Jake, me, and the two points of contact. I turn toward him, but he's already gone.

***

I'm on Tempedral property not far from the building's hidden back door when I hear a sound that makes me freeze. Sweet bloody Janus. I hold my breath and do my best to determine the direction of the scraping noise.

"Somerset," I hear. My mother's voice. I follow it to find her sitting right next to the concealed entryway. Has she known about it all this time? Does she know how often I use it? For a split siren, I feel younger than Monkey.

My mother has pulled an old bench outside and lit some candles. The flickering light illuminates and exaggerates the worry lines on her face.

"I want to talk to you," she says.

"I'm sorry, Mom," I say. I'm in no mood for an argument. "I know I've been horrible lately. I'm sorry. You know, I didn't really mean it when I said it was all your fault."

"Honey," she says. "It's not your fault either."

Her voice is gentle but firm, and something clenched inside me lets go just a little. I sit down next to my mother and she puts her arm around my shoulders.

"Nobody could stop your dad when he had his mind made up. Especially about something so important to him."

"You tried?"

My mother sighs. "There's a lot you don't understand, Somers. It's complicated."

I have a feeling if I press her for more information, she'd do it. Truth? I can't handle anything more today. We're both quiet for a bit.

"How do you know about this exit?" I ask. "It's not even in the blueprints. I looked."

My mother laughs a little. "Your dad showed it to me when we were dating."

"You and Dad *dated*?" I practically yell. "I thought you were both just matched up through the Tempedral."

"Yes, well, we might not have always exactly followed protocols. You'd be surprised."

We both startle as the curfew siren screams its warning.

"We better go in," my mother says. "We've been told that they're going to start drone enforcement again."

She leads me inside, squeezing my hand as we pass through the secret door. Before tonight I just kind of took its existence for granted. For the first time I wonder who installed it and why. Our Tempedral came down to us through Uncle Criss. Before I begin my bedtime scribble session, I'll make a note to ask him about it.

***

A bad dream night. In the morning I stumble down to the kitchen to find that the room is sparkling clean and breakfast has been laid out for us, a platter of packaged Nutribrix and some crackers arranged in the center of the table. Matthew has enlisted Monkey to help him serve cups of water, and she looks happy as she carefully handles the precious liquid.

"Awww, Monkey, Matthew, thank you," says my mother. "Find everything okay?"

"Sure," says my brother. "It's not like it's difficult to find the B-bars. Good thing they don't taste as bad as they smell."

"You know we have it much better than most," says my mother.

"I do know that. Sorry. I'm just …"

"Hungry," finishes my mother. "I understand. There's no sin in talking about it." She pauses and takes a big breath. "Listen, I have had some news. I'm told that our supplies won't be delivered for a while. We're going to have to …"

"To what?" says Matthew.

"We'll have to get in line. At the meal siren."

"Perfect," grumbles Matthew. "Because we have so much spare time around here."

He glares at me. I know what he's thinking, and he's right. I'm still not doing my fair share of Tempedral stuff and the only reason why it isn't more of an issue is because he's been quietly picking up my slack. I ostentatiously point to my uniform to show him that I'm ready for active clerical duty today.

My mother tells Matthew that it could be much worse. Clericals will have separate stations, which will be safer and quicker than the regular lines.

"What's going on?" I ask. "What's changed?"

"I'm not exactly certain yet," says my mother. She puts her hand on Monkey's shoulder and tells us not to worry. "I'll see what more I can find out. In the meantime, chins up. Citizens look to us for an example as well as guidance."

There's a knock at the kitchen door, which is odd; hardly anyone comes in through this small room at the very back of our family living area. I peer through the thick glass of the small security window. It's Serena, and she's covered in blood.

CHAPTER FIVE

I yell for Matthew to take Monkey out of the room and whip open the door. My mother and I whisk Serena inside. My mother rinses a towel in water and uses it to clean Serena's face, while I unstrap her violin case from her back. She never goes anywhere without it, but I can't believe she was able to hold onto it; even the teardrop charm is still there. Serena is sobbing. I hold her while my mother's soft ebony hands do their gentle work. As the blood and dirt wash away, I can see that, thankfully, her wounds aren't serious, though her face is bruised and she has a deep cut on her forehead.

In fits and starts, her story comes out. She was in line getting 'Brix for her family at meal siren when the station abruptly closed down. The hungry crowd went crazy, storming the building, trying to get inside. It turned into a riot. Serena was knocked down and kicked but managed to stay clear of the worst of it. Armed States soldiers arrived just as Serena got away. We were much closer than her home, so she came to us.

She bursts into fresh tears. I've never seen her like this; she's usually tougher than anyone I know. Then it comes to me: She left with no food. My mother helps Serena change into some of my clothes while I gather supplies to take to her place. Unfortunately, we're down to nothing but 'Brix, stale bread, and some potatoes; it'll have to do. I put water in a large jug that was, at some point in its history, filled with orange juice; its molded label is stamped into the plastic and is still legible. I can't imagine it, no matter how many antique flatbooks I read. Real fruit that could be made into real juice.

My mother has to convince Serena to eat something before we leave, and my friend's reluctance to satisfy her own hunger before getting food to her family kills me. Few people ever see this side of her. On our way out, I grab one more thing, the holofilm disc I borrowed from my Uncle Criss. Serena's family shares their house with a bunch of other folks, including friends of Serena's who seem to always be tinkering with electronic projects, most of which have been built from scavenged, outlawed technology. I bet they'll have something we can watch the holofilm on, and her performance on it should do nicely to cheer us up.

Serena is feeling much better. She must be, because she asks for a detour.

"Where to?" I ask.

"Watch and learn," says Serena.

She's definitely feeling better.

***

Foot traffic is sluggish today, the thick air conspiring with a low lemon sky to stupefy even the most rugged among us. A guy near me, who looks like he could dispatch both Serena and I into oblivion with a single flick of his wrist, stops in his tracks and rather daintily fans his face with his hand. The people immediately behind him do everything they can to keep from plowing into him. One woman who makes contact with the back of his cloak gets off with a mere glance rather than a striking blow. It's a welcome byproduct of our collective lethargy.

Eventually I realize that we are heading to what is still known as Oceanside, though I know from antique flatbooks that the water bordering this area is no longer anything close to what the sea once was. I've seen faded images of white-topped cresting blue-green waves, and emerald lagoons that glitter against blue skies. This water bubbles toxic gasses from swirling brown eddies. This water can dissolve a human body within a couple of days.

It's been years since I was near this place. Ruined jetties crawl with scavengers looking for anything of value; strange things have been known to float to the water's venomous surface. Grimly trimming the neighborhood is a desiccated boardwalk, most of its boards gone to provide shelter from the sun. And even out here, holo billboards hawking Reverie. I'm wondering why we've come.

"This'll just take a few minutes," she says, reading my mind. "Okay if I keep your suncap?"

"Sure. You can keep everything you're wearing."

She looks at me. "Thank you," she says simply.

I follow her underneath this weird metal structure stuck in the sand. It has a high ladder that supports a long metal trough that slopes at an angle before it flattens out at the bottom. Heat radiates off this thing, and I hope I don't accidently touch it during whatever is supposed to happen next. It looks like someone lives here.

An older man lopes toward us, his face a leathery map of

lines and wrinkles. He stops, peering at us through sagging, blistered eyelids.

"Serena, my favorite young criminal!"

"Ho!" says Serena, and they shake hands. I am not introduced, and the man doesn't look my way.

"What have you got?" he asks.

Serena removes the suncap from her head. "For two cans of oldtime," she says.

"Deal," says the guy.

I hand him my suncap. "Four cans," I say. He says nothing but takes it, still averting his eyes. He puts the caps underneath his shirt and ambles off into the distance.

The sky seems to turn a more oppressive shade of amber, and just when I think I might collapse under its weight, he returns with the cans of food. Beans and corn.

"'Til we meet again," says the man, mock bowing before Serena.

"In the fullness of time," says Serena, and they both laugh.

We're exhausted by the time we reach Serena's. We flop down on her narrow sleeping pallet in a tiny area separated by a thin filmy curtain. When she carefully places her violin on a ragged pillow, it takes up most of her living space. The sounds of her extended family and housemates envelope us, and I wonder how she, or anyone under this roof, ever sleeps.

"Let me see your forehead," I say, and she pulls back her hair to show me.

"Is it okay?" she asks.

"It's fine," I say. "The mark of Cain becomes you."

"The what of who?"

"Hey," I tell her. "I have a surprise for you."

"Today has been full of surprises," she says. "Don't think I can handle another."

She perks up when I tell her about the concerto disk. She yells for someone named Angus, and he soon appears at her curtain; a perk, I guess, of such close quarters. No privacy at all, but your people are always within earshot. She explains what we need, and within a remarkably short time, we're ready to watch the holofilm on a contraption he's found. We have to scale it way down, but Angus thinks it will work well enough. We're most interested in the audio, anyway. We politely ask Angus if he'd like to watch it with us, but he says no, he'll probably be able to hear it from his room. Which is true, and besides, there's no place for him to sit.

The holofilm opens with an odd visual. The camera's point of view seems to be above and behind Uncle Criss, who's sitting in front of a computer screen in his study. On his screen is footage from Dad's Reverie. There's a close-up of Serena as she begins to play, and my uncle leans forward, maybe to hear better.

Uncle Criss turns his head to look at someone entering the room; all we can see is the shadow of what looks like trousered legs. My uncle gestures for silence until Serena's piece ends. Taft walks into the frame.

UC: "This child, in another time, another place, would have been considered a prodigy. She's my niece's friend. I'm going to see that talent like hers gets recognized. One day."

Taft: "Mnnn … Right. Okay."

UC: "What fresh hell brings you here, Grayson? I thought I made it clear that my home is off-limits."

Taft: "How long have you known?"

UC: "That's a rather awkward question, isn't it? How long in Statestime or real time? In any case, there's no conspiracy that's kept you in the dark. At least, none that I know of. I suspect you've not been keeping up with the reports you've been sent."

Taft: "I've been busy handling the new protocols for the FireSquad. I had no idea things had gotten this bad!"

UC: "You'd better calm down. I've seen your med file and it's almost as frightening as my own."

Taft throws himself into a chair. He starts babbling.

Taft: "First the fossil fuels fiasco, then the heat, then the damn bugs go, now pretty soon, us too."

UC: "Maybe the planet is returning fire, trying to survive its most dangerous animals. Humans have been lethally arrogant. Time to reap what we've sown."

Taft: "What's the latest?"

Uncle Criss presses a button and a holo grid chart appears. I can't make out the numbers.

UC: "The latest."

Taft: "Christ."

Serena gasps. He's just uttered the most serious of the word infractions.

Taft: "There must be some stock holds we haven't tapped yet. Or some new bins dug up?"

UC: "We've been lurching toward this shortfall for a very long time now. It's our good luck that it's going to hit in our lifetime. Ha!"

Taft: "What's our next move here? You and I both know how pathetically ill-equipped we are at this point to handle any mass panic. It'd make these food riots look like a bloody ballet.

UC: "Yes, well. That's what happens when the inmates run the asylum."

Taft: "What did you say?"

UC: "Time to shove off, Grayson. I'll be at the Center tomorrow and we'll continue our discussion then."

Taft: "You MUST have some fancy endgame worked out for you and your family! What have you got planned?"

UC: "There's always Reverie."

Taft, sarcastically: "Right. Of course."

Taft stalks angrily out of the room.

UC: "'And all our yesterdays have lighted fools the way to dusty death.'"

Uncle Criss turns and looks right at us. "Shakespeare," he says. He reaches toward us, and the holofilm disappears. My world tilts madly.

"What the wretched hell was that?" Serena practically squeaks.

My mind is a shiny blank space. I muster the simplest truth available to my brain.

"I think it's a surveillance holo from my uncle's study."

CHAPTER SIX

"We gotta show this to Jake right away," says Serena. "Where does he live?"

"I don't know," I say. Serena looks skeptical. "I really don't. We haven't gotten to that point."

"Okay then, what next?"

"I think I know where to find him. Let's go." I grab the disk. Serena nods grimly and follows me. She's not happy when I tell her where we're going.

"The Fallows, are you kidding? I can't picture you there. Even Stone avoids that place."

"You don't need to worry about me." And I mean it. I was trained to use an e-tazyr when I was fourteen. I've never yet had to use it, but it's good to know I have it.

It's a trek getting there. We have plenty of time to take in the scenery: blasted, formerly wooded dustlands, faded garden sheds turned into bartering shops, makeshift lean-tos, old cars, and wheeled machines now housing families, even a tired-looking Reverie Kiosk. 'Brix wrappers drift across and around dead vegetation. These wrappers are the one thing citizens won't repurpose like everything else; they represent such a universally loathed substance that they are discarded immediately and shunned.

We get closer to the heart of the neighborhood, a strange duo in this place, me in my clerical habit, and Serena in her dun-colored shift, her violin strapped over her back. But nearly everyone seems to be on something or other, slurring their rough speech and staggering around. Nobody targets us. I find what must be the gaming center; Jake's described it to me. We go inside a huge tent which covers a big cement rectangle in the ground where people used to bathe for fun. It smells really bad in here, a noxious mix of human sweat, excrement, and smoke. A small crowd is watching Jake and some others play cards, and we join them. Serena recognizes and waves to a few of the observers, which surprises me not at all; she gets around.

There's a big pile of contraband in the center of the ring of players. Cigarettes, pieces of electronics, canned food, and most unusually, an antique cellphone. Jake deals two cards to each of the four other gamers and himself. Jake's told me about this game. It's called Guts.

The player to Jake's right says he's out. So does the gambler on his left, who I recognize as the teen Jake bartered with. A third guy says, "Yeah. Done. Out."

Attention shifts to the fourth player, a huge hulk of a man. He says he's out. Jake says he's in, and he reaches toward toward the pile of goods. Enormous Dude extends one of his massive arms across the table and his hand forms a stop signal. "In!" he yells.

I know that he can't do this under the rules of Guts from listening to Jake's stories. Jake's face remains impassive, but everyone else looks uneasy. My own heart is beating fast, and Serena is now painfully gripping my upper arm.

"So?" says Enormous Dude. "Whadya got?"

"A proposition," Jake says.

"Huh?" says Enormous Dude.

"Double down?" says Jake.

"What the hell?" says the big man.

"That jewelry you won last time. I'm sure it's on you."

Enormous Dude lifts a necklace out from under his filthy shirt. Dangling from the chain is a glittery cross. The crowd hoots; it's very valuable and very illegal.

Jake says, "Your chain. My …"

Jake reaches into his pocket and pulls out an antique wind-up watch; it looks like the same one I saw when he got his ice. He must have won it earlier. Loud noises come from the crowd. "Time-keeper!" someone yells. Enormous Dude stares hard at Jake. Maintaining his gaze, he rips the chain from his neck and tosses it into the pot. Jake drops the watch on top of it.

Enormous Dude shows his hand. A pair of nines. Jake reveals a pair of queens, and in the same motion, sweeps the prize pile into a burlap sack. Enormous Dude and the spectators appear stunned by the speed of what's just happened. The first three players who withdrew stand and stumble toward the exit.

Jake's opponent looks furious. He stands and leans over the table, his giant head inches from Jake's face.

"Ho, my friend," says Jake.

"You're no friend of mine," says the guy. "Give it back."

Jake says, "Ah. Would that I could."

"Wha … Huh?" says Enormous Dude.

Jake says, "I'd love to. Can't."

"I'll kill you," says the man.

Jake smiles. He rises from the table and positions himself

so that they are face to face. He speaks softly and takes something out of his pocket; I can't see what it is. Jake gestures to the guy, that mocking salute he sometimes does to me. Enormous Dude sways for a split siren; I can almost feel the rage inside this guy roll off him in waves. He turns and leaves, stomping his way out. For some reason, Jake looks up then, and he sees me and Serena. He cocks his head to the side and winks at me. And then, wretched hell, the curfew siren wails.

We all move toward the opening of the makeshift casino. Jakes reaches us quickly and guides us out, elbowing people aside and walking quickly enough that we have to nearly run. We wind up the narrow staircase, Serena's violin case cracking violently against its cement surface. She winces but charges ahead, and the three of us leave The Fallows as fast as we can.

A thought occurs to me. Not a happy one. "Drones," I say out loud. "My mother said they were going to start using the searchbirds again!"

Now we really get going, moving as quietly as possible. By the time we get to the Deadwoods, it's fully dark. Overhead we hear the low buzz that precedes the search drones. We freeze and wait. The sound fades. We've been lucky. My home is closest, and we reach it without any trouble.

I try to convince Jake and Serena to spend the night with me and my family, but they insist on going home. We make a plan to meet in the morning at Wagner's, an old barter salon not far from our Tempedral. Jake asks if either of us will be seeing Stone.

"Serena can give him the message, if she's not too busy," I say, and she makes a rude gesture.

I scurry through the hidden door and rush upstairs, where I find Matthew waiting for me next to the neatly concealed break in the Great Hall's wall mural. Sweet Janus. Does everybody know about this stairwell and exit?

"Bloody hell, you scared me," I breathe.

Matthew takes me by the arm—not gently—and pulls me deeper into the hall, and then into the kitchen.

"Please don't be mad. I promise …"

"Don't make any promises to me I know you won't keep," says Matthew. "And yes, I'm angry! Mom is worrying herself crazy, have you noticed? Luckily, she's with Monkey right now, and I won't tell her about tonight. But I'm mostly worried, Somers. What the heck are you up to? And what makes you think you're exempt from curfew, too?"

"What do you mean, 'too'?" I ask, stalling.

"You've just been *gone* lately! You don't go to Tempedral services, you don't help with chores—half the time, you're not even home for meals. And Monkey! Whatever that kid has been through, she certainly doesn't need to lose you, too."

Truth? This last part hits me hard. But I don't say anything. Matthew gives me a disgusted look. He opens his mouth to say something else but closes it and leaves. I shouldn't let him go without making it right between us, or at least trying to, but I do. The long day has caught up with me, and it's all I can do to get to my room and collapse on my bed, where I obsess over Uncle Criss's holofilm. I don't know which part of the equation to focus on; the content of the holo or my uncle's role in whatever's going on. I can't sleep for a long time.

CHAPTER SEVEN

I'm dressed and out of the house before sunrise; sunrise and sunset, two aspects of the day's rhythms the States can't adjust. I still have time off from school and the Center, but I want to talk to Nan Wilder. On the way over I'll come up with some pretext for seeking her out; what I really want is any light she can shine on Taft's starring turn in my uncle's holofilm, which is in my bag. The foot traffic isn't too bad because it's still so dark and before I know it, I find myself in front of the Center retscan without a reasonable excuse for talking to Nan. I'll wing it.

I get through the first scan quickly, but there's a delay at the second; I have to scan both eyes before I'm admitted beyond the reception area. It's never happened before, and it kind of spooks me. Not a good omen. When I reach my tiny intern's cubicle, I'm startled by the sound of someone moving around nearby. I follow the noise to Nan's office. I knock, and she gestures for me to come in. She doesn't even ask me why I'm there; she just thrusts a HydraTablet at me and asks me to provide her with a summary.

I'm about to ask what I hope will be subtle but productive questions when Taft stops in front of Nan's office door and then barges in. "What a lovely surprise," he says to Nan. He doesn't acknowledge me. "You've been resuscitated early this morning."

"Shouldn't you still be in Gennestown?" asks Nan.

"Shouldn't you still be on oxygen? What are you doing here?"

Nan shrugs. "Do you not complain incessantly about the lack of progress in the West End? And technically, I'm a civilian, prohibited from having tech at home. So, I'm here."

"I would have thought you'd have rigged up something for yourself by now," says Taft.

Nan answers with exaggerated patience, like she's talking to a child. "You forget how the other half lives, Grayson. I share a place with fourteen other people. So not only would that be illegal, it'd be ridiculous. It'd be shredded for parts within hours."

Taft finally looks at me. "Are you back?" he barks. And then he stomps out without waiting for an answer.

"Are you? Back?" says Nan.

"Not all the way," I say. "I wonder if we could talk?"

"Absolutely," says Nan. "But not now. I'll meet you here tomorrow at midday siren. Will that work for you?"

I nod, and Nan goes back to whatever it is she's doing. I need to meet my cell, so I check out of the building and stuff my clerical uniform in my bag. I'm nearly at the meet spot when hunger hits me hard. There's probably one of the new clerics' stations somewhere nearby, but I don't want to waste time having to find it. After a short wait in line, I'm able to buy two B-bars at a regular station. I'm so hungry by then I don't even mind the taste; they are unusually awful, even for 'Brix. They must be pretty old.

I'm last to arrive at Wagner's. Serena has told Jake and Stone about the holofilm, and they're anxious to see it. Jake has gone somewhere to find something we can show it on. Then he comes back with a device that looks cobbled together from what are probably many generations of cannibalized machines. It doesn't currently resemble anything that could possibly be useful. It takes a while, but Jake is able to coax the thing into action. He gives me a swashbuckling salute, and it's kind of adorable how pleased he is with himself. I brace myself for a second screening as the holo is set up in a dark corner of the salon.

Stone watches with his mouth slack and open the entire time; when the holo ends, Serena leans over, cups her hand beneath his chin, and closes it for him. Jake starts to curse and yell, and we have to quiet him down and remind him that we're in public. I put my arm around his shoulder and across his back, and he looks at me with surprise. This is the most physical we've ever been with each other. It seems to calm him, though. I watch as his face hardens into an expression I remember from watching him gamble. Focused. In his element.

Jake tells us to prepare for an emergency action later. "Not a poetry reading, Somerset," he says meanly. I'm surprised, and I wonder if I crossed a line with my hug. He tells us to find somewhere to rest until two sirens, find something to eat, and prepare for an active evening. Jake stalks away to wherever he goes to recharge; I can't imagine what that might look like. Serena leaves with Stone. And I leave for a section of the city called Voxx, where the closest 'Brix manufacturing plant is located. I want to follow up on a hunch.

I need to conserve my energy for the action, so I do

something I don't ordinarily; I pay for a cart. I do take the precaution of waiting for a driver that looks like they won't slit my throat, an older woman who looks physically strong and independent of mind. A rainbow-colored band holds back her graying-red hair, and despite the heat, she wears an extra layer, a flowy colorful fabric that swirls around her neck and down over the back of her shoulders.

Turns out, she's a talker. She calls herself Aurora. She says she renamed herself when she was a young woman in response to a beautiful sunrise she shared with her first love, a non-gendered personage named Ramsey. She has a flask with her that she keeps tucked behind the small of her back and draws from it frequently.

"Ramsey and I," the woman sighs, "what a time we had. We were going to find someplace different and build a home together. They were technically gifted, though, and they eventually were 'recruited' to work in the Government Center. It was the end of us. But I dream of them still. I wish them nothing but happiness. It would be wonderful to see them before I go."

"Go where?" I ask.

"Wherever," says Aurora. "I'll find out."

"Not choosing to rev?" I say.

She laughs. "I was born a cleric."

I'm so surprised that I'm completely rude. "Wretched bloody hell!" I gasp.

"Hard to picture, I know, but it's true. Here," she says, thrusting her flask in my direction. Truth? She misses her mark by a wide margin, and I hope I haven't made a mistake trusting her to drive me. I reach for the bottle and take a companionable sip. Sweet Janus, the stuff is just awful.

Worse than 'Brix. I will myself to swallow it down rather than embarrass myself by spitting it out over the side of the cart.

"What happened?" I ask.

"I lost my faith. Then I lost my tribe," says Aurora. The look she gives me makes me want to cry.

***

The factory is massive, its noise deafening. I tear a precious page out of the notebook in my bag and make myself earplugs. When I get closer, I notice something strange. These factories are notoriously well-guarded, but as I scope out the nearest entryway, I can't see anyone. I scale the fencing and creep closer. Nobody. Then I hear voices. I tiptoe around a corner and see four or five armed soldiers. All drunk, sprawled in the dirt, throwing dice. I'm elated; the factory retscan should allow me in as an official employee of the Government Center. I'm not supposed to be here, but unless somebody has a reason to check the records, I should be okay.

The first thing I notice when I'm inside is that it's hotter in here than outside. This is just wrong; all these plants are supposed to be carefully temperature-controlled. That's nothing compared to my next shock. The vast interior of the place is deathly still. No moving conveyor belts, no automated package sealing, nothing. I find a storage area, and another, and a third. All empty of the B-bars they're supposed to house. What I can't figure out is the noise. I make my way across the sticky flooring to a big room that looks like a deserted office and look around. Wretched hell. The sounds emanating from this dead factory are recordings pumped through huge speakers to the outside.

My heart starts hammering. As the enormity of what I've discovered starts to hit me, I'm panicked at the thought of being caught in here. I retrace my steps and ease open the same door I used to get in. No one seems to have resumed their sentry. I slip through the entryway and race toward the fencing, where, sweet Janus, someone is waiting for me: my uncle Criss.

He watches me scale the rotted barrier without extending any help or words of encouragement. It's one of the things I've always loved about him, his absolute faith in my abilities, such as they are. He waits until I have two feet on the ground before speaking.

"I've been waiting for you to explore the premises," he says dryly.

"But how …?" I begin.

"I've been monitoring your retscans," he says. Ah. My brain cannot come up with a single response to this information. As we start to walk, the driver of the States car he came in slowly follows us. "First things first. What did you make of your Experience?"

Not what I expected. I blurt out the first thing that comes to mind. "I didn't want to come back here."

My uncle nods. "And yet, my dear, here we are. It's not yet your time."

"How does anyone know?" I ask. "How did Aunt Stella know?"

"Well, that was an unusual situation. She was very ill. For her, it was less a calling than an option with a limited window of opportunity. I know you've never heard much about those days."

"No," I say. I find myself holding my breath. I have no recollection of my aunt.

"No one talks about it. I did a shameful thing. It wasn't yet my time for Reverie, but … I went with her. I was very … distraught. But I came back."

"What are you talking about? No one comes back!" I'm stunned.

"That's not entirely true," says Uncle Criss. "It's not a well-known or at all publicized fact, but it happens sometimes. Usually it's because of a procedural error. After I administered The Gift to Stella, I gave it to myself. I was in great pain, and I must have made some mistakes; it's a delicate process. But also, I struggled against it. I regretted my course of action nearly instantaneously. It wasn't my time. And so, I came back. For our family, and for a greater good."

My mind is reeling, and when my uncle's HydraMobile goes off, at first, I think the ringing sound is inside my head. He looks at it and sighs.

"Taft," he says. "You know how he is. A very dramatic type."

"He's a psychopath," I say.

"A prerequisite for the job. I must go, but we'll talk again soon, my dear." He puts me in his car and tells the driver to take me anywhere I'd like. As we pull away, I look back at my uncle in time to see a translucent helicopter descend noiselessly and land near him. His white hair flies around his face as he waits for an attendant to help him inside.

***

I know this driver. His name is McInnes, and he's actually more of a bodyguard than a wheelman. He never says much, but I always feel safe around him. He lets me off near the agreed-upon meet spot, a cart station in the heart of the city, for tonight's action. He doesn't ask any questions, but he says he'll wait for a bit before he leaves, in case I need him. He's not somebody you argue with.

I walk toward the station, prepared to wait; I'm early, I think. Then I see it, the number *147* scrawled into the graffiti on a dilapidated bench: This action's been called off. Glad I didn't try to dissuade him from waiting for me, I ask McInnes to take me home. The next thing I know, we're stopped at the Tempedral, and he's gently calling my name; I've been asleep. I'm groggy and I just sit for a split siren.

"Are you feeling all right, Ms. Whitman?" asks McInnes.

I mumble something, and he helps me out of the car. As we walk to the Great Hall's front doors, they open and a small pale figure hurls itself at me.

"Somerset, you're home! You're just in time!" cries Monkey.

"In time for what?" I laugh. "What have you been up to?"

"Cooking," she shrieks.

"Really," I say. "With what?"

"Nutribrix! They melt! I'm making them into cookies. Come have some!" says Monkey.

"Yum," says McInnes, with a marked lack of enthusiasm. "I wish I could stay, Miss, but if Ms. Whitman is feeling better?" He looks at me, and I nod. "Thank you, but I'm afraid I must get back to work."

"Coward," I whisper as he leaves. And the corner of his mouth lifts just the tiniest bit.

Monkey pulls me inside. I tell her about how tired I'm feeling, that I'm going to change clothes and rest, and that I'll see her at supper. She runs back into the kitchen, and I hear her tell Matthew that I'm home and I'll be down soon.

When I reach my room, the door is ajar. I never leave it

open and try to remember if I left anything incriminating out in the open. My mother sits on my bed and, wretched bloody hell, she's got my Plexie wolf mask in her lap. I slump down next to her. I don't know what's wrong with me; I feel all loose and wavy.

"You're one of the elusive mad poets brigade?" she says. "I thought you were keeping a journal."

"It started out like that, but then things changed," I say.

My mother nods slowly. "I've always wondered," she says, "Why a wolf?"

"We're trying to wake up the sheep," I say.

"Ah. And how do you know where and when to gather?" she asks.

"You really want to know?" I say. She nods. "The holo billboards. We have somebody on the inside. Whenever a new one goes up, there are always two versions, a regular one and a special one. When an event is scheduled, that person utilizes the special one. It looks exactly like the other holo, but it has a code embedded in it, if you know where to look in the image. Our programmer can change its message as needed. I'm not sure who they get instructions from; it's an anonymous … club," I finish. I leave out the fact that our cell deploys this same means of communication.

"Club," repeats my mother.

So far, she's handling all this better than I ever could have expected. But I'm not surprised at what she says next.

"You look exhausted. Take a nap and I'll wake you for supper. But Somerset. Please hold off on participating in another … *event* for a week or two. Please. I'm hearing a lot of strange chatter. Please promise me this."

"I promise," I say. And I mean it. It's one of the least

dangerous things I do, safer then say, breaking into a ghost 'Brix factory.

My mother gentles my hair back and smooths my bed-top mesh over me. She starts to hum my favorite lullaby, one about scarlet ribbons and a miracle.

I awaken slowly, then all at once as the memory of my day's labors rushes back to me. As I move toward the kitchen, I can hear the familiar sounds of my abbreviated family; it's a shock every time we're together that my dad isn't among us.

"Did you have a good sleep?" asks Monkey.

"Yes," I say. "How about you? All good?" I ask Monkey, but I look from her to Matthew. Who smiles back. Who's too sweet to ever hold a grudge or believe anyone irredeemable.

"Uncle Criss was here! He found us some eggs and cheese and bread. The cheese is real!" says Monkey.

"Wow!" I say. I look at my mother, who shrugs, and shakes her head. As in, don't know and better not to ask.

We all sit down and have an unusually satisfying and peaceful meal. For a while.

"Somers, Uncle Criss's visit wasn't purely social. He had some advice for us." My mother looks uncomfortable but presses on after glancing at Monkey. "It seems you got lost and wandered into a government facility, yes?" Now she glances at Matthew.

"Yup," I agree.

"Uncle Criss has done his best to excuse your inquisitive nature to the officials, and to highlight your spotless service record at Randall and the Government Center …"

Matthew interrupts my mother by bursting into incredulous laughter. He chokes it back, and I give him my patented-from-childhood Death Stare.

"We're not sure why the retscan was monitored," says my mother. "But we need to be very careful now. The talk at the last clerics' assembly was somewhat unusual. I'm not quite sure what's going on, but we may be in for more changes."

My brother clears his throat. "Um … I should say something. Maybe I should have earlier, but I didn't want to worry anyone needlessly. I was notified that Somerset had attracted some comments when Dad's Reverie footage came through. All the heads of clerical households were. I'm sorry, Mom, it came to both of us, and I censored yours. I didn't want to add to everything else you've got on your mind."

My brother did something less than honest. For me. I've broken Matthew.

"Why did she get tagged?" says my mother.

"When she … when she fell. It's unusual. I responded right away. I told them it was joy, not … anything else, but apparently there was some discussion because of the increase in demonstrations and sabotage, and the Kiosk numbers. Which have since rebounded a bit, but still. There's a good amount of paranoia now at the G.C."

I stare at my kind, smart older brother. He looks so much like my dad, dark, broad-shouldered, and lanky. And an innocent, such an innocent. Like my dad. True believers, both. I put my arms around him and hug with all my might.

"I'm so sorry I got you caught up in this," I begin.

"I'd do anything for you, for all of you," he says simply. "Please be more careful."

I nod. And then, as calmly as I can, I tell them about what I found in the 'Brix plant. My mother closes her eyes and rubs her forehead. Matthew gasps when I come to the part about the recorded manufacturing sounds being pumped outside to maintain the illusion of industry. Then we are all quiet, except for Monkey, who is singing softly while arranging and rearranging bits of her bread and egg.

"I hate to bring this up now," says my mother, "but we need to discuss Decemberday. They've let us know; it's in two days."

"We are not going to that wretched party!" I yell.

"We especially need to go now, Somers, don't you see?"

"Lord!" I spit out.

"Somerset!" Matthew yells. He looks around like he's forgotten we're in our private quarters. No cameras. No witnesses.

"You will," says my mother. "We will all go. We'll go, we'll present ourselves, open to public scrutiny, we will mingle, and we will leave. Monica, I have a new habit for you!"

"Monkey!" says the small girl.

"And Monkey you will remain," says my mother.

"Because I can hold on!" says Monkey.

"Because you can hold on," says my mother. "We will all hold on!" she says, looking at Matthew and me. "But this is a very fancy party, and we will use our formal names, okay? At the party, you'll be Monica, if you please."

"That's good with me," says Monkey. "Who wants some cookies?"

CHAPTER EIGHT

Decemberday. The only Government-sanctioned holiday of the year, held at the discretion of said offices, at a time they deem appropriate. Sometimes it's announced way in advance and sometimes we find out when the Tempedral bells all ring at once, and everything just comes to a stop. It's always seemed to me that Decemberday occurs when Taft and company determine the peasants most need to blow off some steam. Officials distribute extra food, water, and spirits to States citizens, and everybody pollutes as many brain cells as possible. This means lots of fights, fires, and other assorted mayhem. Officials and clerics must attend an elaborate celebration and put on a show of strength and loyalty. It's excruciating. This year, I don't know how I'm going to manage it.

Matthew gets word that Nan Wilder has canceled our appointment; the Center has closed but she'll see me at the D-Day gala, she says. My brother tells me that Randall has also shut down until two days after the holiday, which is typical. I'd like to keep Monkey away for even longer. We'll see. Maybe this year will be calmer than last year; at its apex drunken citizens burned Taft in effigy, along with a couple of States trucks. All signs, though, point to an especially tumultuous occasion: food down, tempers up, heat blistering.

The next few days will be relatively quiet around here; usually, the number of citizens considering Reverie dives during the festivities. Nobody bails before Decemberday extras, and my family can relax a little. Monkey and I go out for a walk on the grounds, do some reading lessons, and then join my mother and Matthew for a small meal.

After our food, I sneak out; the walking path I took with Monkey just happened to feature a view of the holoboard that looms over the west wall of our grounds. Its coded instructions told me that our cell has a meeting in the city. I leave in full uniform so as not to agitate any camera monitors; I'll find a place for a quick change when I'm a less visible target.

My first stop is a tree we sometimes use in the Deadwoods. It's cracked on one side, and the resulting wooden slot is perfect for the low-tech kinds of messages our cell likes to use. I'm directed to a place I've never heard of called the TOC. No idea what it stands for. The Deadwoods is a great place to ditch my habit, and I sling it into my bag, replace my headdress with a suncap, and move on.

The TOC turns out to be a small necessities shop tucked into a corner of a residential neighborhood. I'm examining the weird makeup they have, holding a bottle up to my face to check for compatibility, when Jake speaks from behind me.

"Not your shade. Try this," he says, placing a tube of some stuff against my cheek, which I can feel become hot with embarrassment. Damn, but isn't the boy correct. He's chosen a perfect color called Raisin. SPF 1,550.

I can't stop him from buying it for me. "What kind of recon is this?" I ask.

"I may have misled you there," he says, grabbing the purchase and my elbow at the same time. "We're not actually meeting as a cell today. Just me and you."

"Umm …" I say. Yeah, I'm just that quick on my feet. For a split siren, I think I may bolt. But then, Jake smiles at me and the full force of it reminds me a little of the feelings that surfaced during my Experience.

"I want to show you where I live," he says. "It's a walk. Maybe an extra veil?"

"I've got one in my bag. I've got a couple, actually. Here," I say.

Jake takes the veil I hand him and instead of draping it over his suncap, he winds it around his face. He suggests I do the same.

"You ever hear of a Lost Ages thing called a mummy?" I ask.

"Sure," he says. "Also, some wretched great flatfilms star mummies. I loved those."

"You've seen a lot of them? Flatfilms?" I say.

Jake says, "At Camp. I'm sure you did, too."

I'm stunned. "You went to Camp? What years?"

"Too many," he says. "I stayed on as a counselor." He starts laughing. "Why Miz Whitman. I do believe I've managed to astonish you," he says in a fakey drawl.

"I never figured you for a Camp type," I confess.

"Most people wouldn't. Especially now. But I showed what, at the time, they called 'promise' and was given license to mingle with the temprats and officials' kids. A real honor for someone who grew up the way I had. Didn't turn out as they planned, I'm sure."

"Yeah," I say. "Most campers are anesthetized by the time it's over. Why do you think they showed us so many flatfilms? I always thought that was strange. Kind of counterproductive, you know?"

"I've thought about that, too. They worked us hard. I think it was just the cheapest way they could think of to entertain the slave labor. I also think none of them had the imagination to understand how powerful those things could be or how we might find them provocative. They just dismissed them as antique kids' toys, you know, because they're flat and creaky."

"I loved them," I say.

"Yeah. Just the deuce. The mosquito-terrorized world flickering against our eyeballs for sirens. Those were the days."

"And nights," I say.

"Do tell," says Jake.

"I'm into full disclosure. It was when I was a counselor. He was the arts instructor. Graham. I was philosophy. We were a good match for a while."

"Until? But then? If only?" says Jake.

"All of those, eventually," I say.

"So, your current status is unencumbered?"

"I wouldn't go that far," I say. "I've got lots of bad habits."

"Such as?"

"I have a really hot temper. I avoid any situations where I'll be called upon to do even very simple math. And I will too often make the hard choice, just to prove something to myself."

"In my experience, the hard choice is usually the right one," Jake says.

In slow motion, he leans over and kisses me through my veil on the lips. He tastes like salt and smoke.

Jake's place looks very strange. It's a fragment of some sort of very old commercial building made of flaking concrete blocks. Remnants of its original signage are barely visible across its side, black circles and faded red letters. Jake uses an antique key to open a heavy metal door.

"You know what this used to be?" he asks as we enter.

"Is this … was this a bowling alley?"

"Very impressive!" Jake says. He takes my hand and leads me to a wall shelf. There are dozens of bowling balls lined up in assorted colors; it's one of the most beautiful things I've ever seen. The space is full of surprises. Some of the lanes are still intact, and judging from the mess, Jake uses one of them for sleeping. There's an ancient radio set and a Hydra on a desk. There's other cool stuff, too, but none of these wonders compares to what I see next.

"Bloody hell," I breathe as a scrawny cat walks toward me. I just plop down on the floor with the enormity of it, blood rushing to my head and crashing rhythmically in my ears. I've never seen a real one before.

"How are you allowed to let it live?" I ask, stroking its fur as it flattens itself against my leg.

"Define 'allowed,'" says Jake, sitting down next to me. "Her name is Betsy. She may be the last living cat in the States, I don't know."

Betsy jumps into my lap, and I get a lump in my throat. She looks up at me with huge gray eyes while I pet her ribs, sadly pointy and prominent. She weighs next to nothing but purrs happily under my touch; I guess she wouldn't have survived this long if she couldn't adapt to circumstances.

She licks my hand and, just like my flatbooks said it would be, it's warm, rough, and lovely. A wave of grief for all things lost washes over me and nearly pulls me under.

I don't know how many sirens go by while I play with Betsy. And with Jake. Eventually, the real world intrudes in the form of hunger. Jake has some 'Brix and water, which we share with Betsy. Over our meal, I tell him about the comatose food plant and the elaborate audio ruse. Pooling the information from my work at the Government Center, my uncle's holo, and my most recent adventure brings us to an unwelcome conclusion. Something is coming to a head, fast. Something bad.

"What are you thinking about your uncle?" asks Jake.

"I don't know. There's so much there … He got me the job with Taft. He's always been there for me and my family. I just don't know where he stands. But I love him, and I've always trusted him."

"I've trusted a lot of people," says Jake. "Hasn't always worked out well."

"Don't worry about me," I say. He wraps me in his arms, and I close my eyes.

***

Our annual preparations for Decemberday take up the next day. Everything must be cleaned, polished, and cooled; traditionally, before the big party, all Tempedrals are subject to an official inspection to make sure they are properly enticing. We use up most of our lightning rations for the year on these occasions. When we finish our work, my mother, Matthew, Monkey, and I luxuriate in the chilled air. Serena stops by at my invitation, and we all have a blissful, picnic-style meal in the Great Hall, where the temperature is a frosty eighty-three degrees. The best is when Serena takes out her violin and plays happy, fast tunes on it while we all dance. Then she plays a slow song, a waltz she calls it, and we all take turns teaching Monkey how to glide along with a partner.

"You are a wonder, Serena," says my mother. "How long has your violin been in your family?"

"I'm actually not sure how many years," says Serena. "But a very long time. My da taught us all to play when we were little, but it was me that stuck with it. Da says it's always like that; in every generation there's a musical nail that sticks up. Then it's our job to not be hammered down. And we have to protect the violin. Which means I never let it out of my sight."

"Well, it's our good luck to have the pleasure of both your friendship and your considerable talent," says Matthew.

Serena catches her breath, and she looks quickly away from my brother. I didn't think the girl was capable of such a delicate show of emotion. I catch her eye and go cross-eyed, and she throws an empty 'Brix carton at me.

My mother insists that Serena take an official clerical car home as the streets are already worse than usual. After promising to come right back afterward, I get in the car with her to keep her company. We pull up to the front of her house, and I can't believe my eyes. Stone is out front, drinking something out of a can with several of Serena's housemates, including one of her brothers. This is sub-optimal. It's unusual enough that Serena and I were allowed to be in the same cell, and not at all good that Jake and I might lately be caught together outside cell-driven activities.

That Stone is waiting for Serena at her residence is plain off-the-charts reckless. Everything is coming apart.

Serena looks at me, and I know we're both thinking the same thing: What now? She hugs me goodbye and casually enters her house alone. Stone leans over and says something to her brother, who slaps him on the back and laughs, and makes a big show of inviting Stone inside. And I'm driven away, back to the Tempedral, where I know I'll obsess about Stone until I have answers.

I don't have a lot of time to ruminate after I get home, though. The inspection occurred in my absence, and it's time to prepare for the traditional Decemberday feast. Usually we have a bunch of guests, but in this post-Reverie year, my mother has asked only Uncle Criss and McInnes. Monkey spends a lot of time at Uncle Criss's, and she loves them both. She's racing around like a maniac, and I wonder if she'll have the stamina for the whole dinner. It's very long and structured. I once read an old flatbook that talked about a Lost Ages holiday called Passover and wondered if there was a connection; the ritualized meal for that celebration reminds me of the D-Day feast. I keep forgetting to ask my uncle about it. Actually, I have a lot of questions for him, all far more pressing than that one.

Monkey is hopping from foot to foot in her excitement, and I take her outside to wait. She draws two figures in the sand. One, I recognize immediately because of his flyaway hair; it's a pretty good rendering of our uncle. I point to the other one.

"Who's this?" I ask.

"That's Monster," says Monkey, still drawing.

"Monster? Who's Monster?"

"You know," says Monkey. "The man who watches me when Uncle Criss is busy."

"Why do you call him Monster?"

"Don't you think he smells like one? And all he ever says to me he does a growl. But he's nice. He lets me play with the light switches. Uncle Criss doesn't like that, but Monster lets me do it as long as he can still see the screen on his Hydra."

"It might hurt his feelings if he heard you call him Monster. His name is McInnes," I say.

"Okay," says Monkey. "Oh look! Here they are!"

McInnes is at the wheel and Uncle Criss sits on the back seat on his HydraMobile. McInnes waits until he's finished his conversation before opening the doors of the vehicle, for which I'm thankful; judging from my uncle's face, it wasn't a pleasant discussion. He's generally very calm and polite, but when angered, he can take the paint off Plexie. Not because he gets loud, but because no one can weaponize the English language like he can. I get my temper from him, I think. Maybe also my obsession with converting my life into words I can put in my notebook.

Uncle Criss and McInnes carry armloads of food and bottles of water. I raise my eyebrows at my uncle; we both know how resistant my parents have been to his largesse. It's one of the things he and my mother still argue about. My uncle shrugs and smiles. My stomach rumbles; I can't deny I'm excited to see what they've brought.

The meal takes forever. Stories must be told. Songs must be sung. Certain traditional dishes are served in a particular order, each stage of the meal signifying a glorious historical step forward toward the Reorganization and the current blissful status quo. But the food is amazing. I close my ears to the rhetoric and luxuriate in sensation. And I think about my dad, about how he should be here, too. He loved these dinners and the continuity of our family line they represented.

As if she can hear my thoughts, my mother raises her glass. We all follow suit, Monkey waving her small cup in the air.

"A toast. To Saul Whitman, of blessed memory," says my mother. "A better man, husband, father, and brother there never was. Our love for you lives on."

***

Later, Uncle Criss asks about our Reverie Kiosk numbers, and Matthew tells him that while our referrals are down a bit, he thinks they'll rebound after the holiday.

"That would be typical, yes," says my uncle. "You may, in fact, see more than the usual uptick."

"Why?" asks my mother.

"New protocols and strategies," says my uncle. "And the new holoboards are proving very effective. Mobile Kiosks should arrive very soon to handle the expected surge. I have the utmost faith in your ability to adjust your counseling techniques as needed."

Matthew nods, smiling. "May we all eventually find our way to The Gift, in the fullness of time."

My mother bows her head. And I want to grab Monkey's hand and run long, fast, and hard. Instead, I slip her another sweet.

"Somerset told us what she found at the B-bar factory. Can you shed some light on what's happening over there?" asks Matthew.

"Shortages. I'm aware of the situation," says Uncle Criss. "As soon as I have a comprehensive evaluation, I'll let all of you know. In the meantime, you may have noticed that McInnes and I arrived with some … extras. This is important. Please rely on this food supply for the time being, rather than on 'Brix. All right?"

"If you insist," I say, and reach for another piece of bread.

The meal concludes so late that we don't even clean up. Before I fall into bed, I look at my gown for tomorrow's dreaded gala. But it's beautiful, I have to confess. An elegant version of my festive habit, it's flowy, long, and exquisitely light. I lay my arm against the fabric; its creamy white hue makes my dark skin look like it's lit up from the inside, like it's glowing. Despite myself, I wish Jake could see me in this dress.

CHAPTER NINE

Annual Decemberday festivities are always held in a secure facility within the Government Center, all fancied up to look like a ballroom. When my family and I arrive at the gala, the religious/political axis is in full swing. A large stage dominates the glittery room, rich crimson drapes framing the proscenium. The place is packed, and Monkey tightens her grip on my hand.

I spy Nan Wilder chatting with a group of Center colleagues and join her, Monkey at my side.

"It does seem that the increased surveillance is having some impact. The numbers of identifieds are way up," says a man I don't recognize.

"I would take issue with those numbers," says Nan. "Monitoring Reveries is something I've opposed from the beginning. It's such an individual experience for everyone involved. I don't think we can accurately identify much more than the stress of extreme emotion and people responding uniquely to it. What looks like dissent may just be …"

The man interrupts Nan, sounding peeved. "Look," he says, flapping a pale wrinkled hand, "if we need to re-educate an extra few while weeding out the terrorists among them, I say it's no big deal."

Nan puts her hand on my shoulder. "I'd like to introduce you all to our intern, Somerset Whitman, and her sister, Monica. Somerset is Saul and Meredith Whitman's daughter, and Criss Alloy's niece. Believe it or not, *she* was tagged at Saul's Reverie. Would you have *her* re-educated?"

The man looks uncomfortable. The others introduce themselves and shake my hand and then Monkey's.

A tall woman speaks up. "I believe we should outlaw citizen breathing veils. They make facial scanning very difficult for us."

A personage I think I recognize from an office near Taft's has joined the discussion. "Outlawing our citizen's veils would make breathing very difficult for them," they say.

The tall woman laughs. "Two birds. One stone."

The group continues this discussion, and Monkey and I move on before the anger in my belly can reach my face. I show Monkey the wonders of the room we're in, the elaborate tapestries covering the walls, the silky gold tablecloths, the shiny vents pumping in cool sweet air.

"It's almost midnight!" shouts someone.

"Says who?" yells another.

There is some nervous, explosive laughter at this. Monkey and I mingle a bit, catching up with kids I've known forever; there's a bond between us temprats that transcends the awkwardness of their clerical orthodoxy and my lack thereof. They're good people, just brainwashed.

When we join the rest of our family at our table, Uncle Criss is holding court, the old gentleman mobbed by admirers. He waves them away as the midnight chimes begin and the lights are dimmed. The heavy stage draperies part and reveal a gigantic ornate clock face, its hands pointed straight up.

It's the same every year, this backdrop. A leering reminder that the States owns time and that individual time-keeping is outlawed. Sirens keep our time. It's not only a show of States power but an attempt to manipulate our appetites by varying the amount of time between citizen meal and work calls. I think it also makes us more compliant; the constant inconsistency of our daily routines messes with us. Keeps us off-kilter. The worst days and evenings are when the air is so bad it's hard to tell where the sun is.

A choir of scruffy children emerge from the wings, led by one of my mother's cleric friends. The man begins to lead them in a song, something with intricate, soulful harmonies. The room stills to listen.

Servers with heaping platters of food for party guests begin to circulate. As one of them passes in front of the choir, I notice a little boy in the front row; he continues to sing but his eyes are locked onto the trays of food. He starts to tremble, and the boy just behind him closes his hand above his friend's elbow. The front row child scrunches his eyes closed and stands still. I can see him trying to behave himself, and I'm holding my breath. In the next moment, he is undone. He wrenches his arm away from his friend's grip and makes a mad dash off the stage. He lunges into a server, whose tray topples to the ground. In a split siren, the entire choir launches itself toward the spilled food. Everybody starts yelling, and it's absolute mayhem. From the audience, I hear mainly expressions of alarm and disgust. Security personnel arrive and drag the kids out of the room, most of them still stuffing food into their mouths as quickly as they can.

It all happens so fast. I check on Monkey. Her face is even

paler than usual, and she looks like she's going to cry. I pull her onto my lap, and my mother puts her arm around the little girl's shoulders. The lights go up, and Grayson Taft takes the stage. As he opens his mouth to speak, Monkey begins to scream. I have no idea what he says to the crowd. In an instant, my mother and my brother are at my side, and I bundle Monkey into my arms. Uncle Criss ushers us out of the hall. I hear him tell an official that the child has been upset by the choir performance before ordering a car for us.

Monkey wails, and I'm unable to comfort her. I rock her back and forth, singing the scarlet ribbons lullaby. The streets are filled with revelers and with trucks continuing to deliver extra 'Brix, water, and alcohol. Our car moves very slowly. Monkey eventually falls asleep, one hand gripping the back of my dress, the other a gentle weight against the Experience brand on the back of my neck. She stays asleep when we arrive home, and as we carry her inside.

I'm too unnerved to go to bed. Matthew and my mother, too. We sit around the kitchen table, and no one says much at first. Matthew looks awful in a way I can't define. Then, I understand. My big brother is confused, conflicted by what he's just seen. I've never seen him anything less than perfectly comfortable in his own skin.

"Lord," my mother says finally.

"Holy Christ," I say, practically at the same time.

Matthew smiles. "You two are more alike than you know."

"Bloody hell to that," I say, and then we're all laughing, the kind of laughing that'll turn into crying if you let it.

"So, Monkey recognized Taft," I say when we calm down.

"It wasn't just the choir kids and what happened?" asks Matthew.

"She was as upset as we all were," I say. "But when she saw Taft, well, that was something completely different. She knows him."

"Did he see her?" my mother asks me.

"No, I don't think so. But I can't be sure."

"Why," asks Matthew. "What are you thinking?"

"I'm thinking that Monica will stay home for a bit, even after the holiday ends, until we get to the bottom of this," says my mother. "And she'll remain in our private family quarters. Stay clear of the Tempedral areas, agreed?"

Matthew and I don't need to be persuaded.

When I wake up the next morning, Monkey lies in bed with me, her form a small crescent on top of my meshing. I don't want to disturb her, but I'm very hungry and thirsty. I try to slip out from under the bed top as gently and quietly as possible, but she startles awake. When she sees me, she relaxes and grins. Which surprises me.

"Still holding on, Monkey?"

"OOH OOH HAH HAH!" she sings and laughs.

I tie her fuzzy pale braids into a knot on top of her head and pronounce her ready for breakfast. She bounces up and puts her sandals on. Sweet Janus. It's like last night never happened. When we get to the kitchen, I cheerfully inform everyone how hungry we both are, and behind Monkey's back, shake my head and hold my finger to my lips. And it's an ordinary meal, with no mention of the evening before. After last night's display, I can't bring myself to eat the delicacies Uncle Criss gave us, and I unobtrusively opt for 'Brix instead. Afterward, I take Monkey for a walk on our grounds. The holoboard has a new message for me: a level-5 action, one we've already discussed and planned. A dangerous and large effort, involving several cells. Tonight.

I'm still dying to talk to Serena and find out what's up with her and Stone. Why was he at her house? I leave Monkey with my mother, dress in my civilian cottons, and head to Serena's. It's the kind of long walk I'm used to. I find these foot journeys inspire a lot of ideas that get processed through my journaling; usually I'm so preoccupied with these thoughts that I forget to feel tired. I'm extra careful, though; it's the day after Decemberday and, typically, citizens are not at their best, excesses having taken their toll, and festivities are not yet over. My plan: Keep my suncap low and, as always, keep a quick pace.

I'm about halfway there when I start to feel sun-bothered and woozy. There's a rock outside what I hear used to be a theater, where children are playing, and I sit down to rest. I watch as the kids form a circle in the dirt. They hold each other's hands and begin to chant.

"Easy peasey lemon squeezy
Make my burden light and breezy.
We go in, we don't come out.
Everybody! Twist and shout!
Easy peasey lemon squeezy
Make my burden light and breezy.
Go!"

The kids start to flail and shake each other's hands, trying to get the others to let go. I played this game when I was young. It hits me that I never really paid attention to the words before. They strike me now as overtly sinister.

I resume my trek to Serena's, latching on to the tail end of a large group blustering its way through the foot traffic in a snake-like pattern, stumbling, drinking, and shouting. I feel something move beneath one of my feet, and I'm down.

Oh sweet Janus, I'm down!

The taste of sand against my tongue. The world goes dark.

I'm being carried. The world swirls nearly back into focus, and I hear Jake's voice. Then nothing.

***

When I awaken, I don't know where I am. Someplace cooled and filled with electronics. My head begins to clear, and the door opens. McInnes walks in and tells me that my uncle has asked me to rest until he returns home. He tells me not to touch the bandage on my arm and leaves. I look at the careful dressing someone has created, and the sight of it reminds me of my dad. When Matthew and I were little, it was always our dad who attended to our cuts and bruises; he had a talent for it. I start to cry, the full weight of my loss pressing so hard against my ribcage I can barely breathe. I can't seem to stop.

Uncle Criss is at my side when I wake up again. "Mom?" I start.

"I've let everyone know that you're here. A bit battered, but safe."

"What happened?"

"You stopped moving, Somerset. And in an unfortunate neighborhood. Luckily, help arrived in time."

"Help? Who? No one knew where I was," I say.

"I've been keeping track of you, dear, as closely as I can. It was tough to reach you quickly, given the state of the streets today of all days, but you're going to be just fine. A doctor has already come and gone; he examined you and gave you a very mild sedative. Plus rehydration and intravenous nutrition; that's the bandage. Tell me, did you eat any 'Brix today?"

"Wha ... 'Brix? Yes, why?"

My uncle's face tightens. "Don't do it again."

"I don't understand," I say.

"Just don't do it. And remind everyone else not to do it either. I need to fly to Metro West, Somers. I'm so sorry, but I can't cancel. I'm sending you home in a car. Go through the front of the Tempedral to get to your private quarters. Yes?"

I nod. I'm guessing he wants my arrival logged in via camera.

"I want you to stay there until I send McInnes for you tomorrow after midday siren. If McInnes isn't behind the wheel, don't get in the vehicle. We'll talk then. Again, I'm sorry. But I need to go now for all our sakes."

McInnes takes me home. He's as chatty as usual, meaning we drive in silence the whole way, stopping and starting and weaving and dodging citizens staggering through the city. I enter through the Tempedral front gates, as I said I would, but it's probably the only promise I'll manage to keep today. Tonight is the level-5, and I have no intention of letting my cell down. I'll just have to be particularly inventive so as not to be tracked.

When I arrive at the Tempedral, it's full of activity, weird for just one day past Decemberday. My mother races toward me and gives me a hug. I assure her I'm fine; I was just in the wrong place at the wrong time, but I've been given full medical clearance. After a few minutes of fussing, she calms down. She asks me to help Matthew and her with preliminary interviews for Reverie counseling, which I hate, and always do my best to subtly sabotage. Silly, but it makes me feel better, as though my entire life hasn't been about familial complicity.

My first interview is with a middle-aged couple. They are typical Seekers. Neither makes eye contact with me nor initiates any conversation. Huddled together on a bench, their hands are clasped so tightly together that their knuckles are white with the strain. They look only into each other's eyes as they answer the queries on my form.

Most of what the States officials want to know is basic information so that they can keep track of population numbers and demographics. They look for marketing feedback, as well, so that they can replicate their most successful campaigns and revise others that aren't working so well. The couple, Britain and Beck, speak in low voices. They hesitate only once, when I ask about children. "No children," says Beck.

The final question asks why they are seeking Reverie now. "Beck is very sick," says Britain, and he starts to cry. These two break my heart. Their misery is so palpable I don't even try to undermine their determination to rev. I have nothing to offer them if they don't.

My second interview is with an older personage, someone I know and have always liked. Davis runs a small stall in the center of the city from which they dispense lotions, ointments, and, on the down low, spiritual advice. These sessions had always been rumored to be borderline unlawful, and as soon as I was old enough to travel on my own, I made an appointment with them for a talk. It was fun. Davis is the sort of person who soothes through their very presence. I found their company bolstering and understood why so many sought out their guidance. They said nothing radical. Instead, Davis offered me practical strategies for dealing with the tribulations of everyday life, delivering laser-sharp attention to the details I'd given them. They elevated close listening to a form of art. I am shocked that they want to rev.

The meal siren interrupts us. Davis declines my invitation to join my family and me in the kitchen, preferring to stay in the Great Hall and eat the food they've brought for themself. When I return from a quick meal, Davis is gone.

The pace never lets up, and everybody stays very busy. Even Monkey contributes, handing out States flyers, artists' renditions of what citizens can expect post-Reverie. It's sickening. My anger starts to build, and I stoke it, a tight ball of fire in my gut that I'll draw upon tonight for fuel.

***

Jake, Serena, and Stone stand in alarm when I approach them at our meet-up site; this time, it's behind a sagging hut near what used to be a shopping mall.

"Ho, my friend!" yells Jake. "Your business here?"

I pull off my double-layered veil and suncap and do a mocking twirl in my brother's best civilian suit and shoes.

"Wretched hell," says Serena. "Good job."

"I rocked a dress once," says Stone, sitting back down in the dust. "Much cooler in the heat. Easier to pee, too. But it kept catching on stuff."

Jake angles his head at me, and I follow him to a spot a few feet away from the others.

"You're not supposed to be here!" he hisses.

I'm confused.

Five people of various shapes and sizes emerge from the rubble nearby, and whatever Jake is going to say next is postponed. We trot back to the group, and Jake introduces us to our cohorts for the action, a group he calls The Tasmanians.

"Ante up," says Jake, and he starts drawing in the dirt and talking; low-tech leaves no digital residue. The Tasmanians don't say much. They leave us with a knapsack of tools and disappear as soundlessly as they arrived. Jake and I divide the tools between us, and I change into the clothes I brought with me, a flowery shift with a huge fake belly I've sewed into the front. Serena and Stone take off, and it's time for the show.

Our target is the Government Central Warehouse, and it's crowded outside the gates, as usual. Jake and I make our way to front slowly, avoiding interaction with anyone. Once up front, I address an armed guard.

"Do you have a relief room we can use? I really, REALLY need one," I mew piteously.

"Sorry," says the guard. "This area is restricted."

"Please? I'm seven months along and I can't seem to stop …"

Jake puts his hand on the guy's shoulder. "You'll really want to let her use the crapper, unless you want what's gonna happen baked into your brain if she can't, for like, forever. The smell alone will make 'Brix a pleasant memory. Not a scene you'll ever be able to erase. I'm her husband, so I know. I've tried. Save yourself."

The man looks utterly disgusted. "Just be quick. The relief stations are around back. I'll wait for you both here."

"Thanks so much!" I grovel.

Jake and I go to the relief stations adjacent to the back of the mammoth warehouse. We scan the area before entering the first one on the right. Once inside, we retrieve motorized screwdrivers from our packs. As quickly as we can, we remove two large metal flooring panels. Jake uses a flashlight and sure enough, we see that someone has constructed a very crude tunnel underneath.

"It was completed just a couple of days ago," Jake whispers. "Let's hope it holds."

I store the fake belly with the rest of my stuff, and we shimmy down the filthy hole. Me first, then Jake. We crawl when we reach a flat section, and eventually, we hit steel sheeting. From our packs, we extract a face shield, a tiny gas tank, and a welding gun. I grab the mask and the welder.

"I got this," I say.

"You've done this before?"

Rather than answer, I adjust the shield over my face and nod, and Jake gives the gun gas. The slab is thicker than I imagined. It's sweaty, stinky, horrible work, but we pause only once to switch places and drink water. The air is nearly unbearable; close, hot, and muddy-tasting, and I don't let myself conjure up any worst-case-scenario mental images.

When we finally remove the slab, we rest for a few minutes. Then we slowly maneuver past the interior wall through the space we've created; we need to be very careful of the entry point's ragged and scorched edges.

We're inside. The place is huge, filled with crated boxes of 'Brix as far as the eye can see. Jake has procured a HydraMobile for this operation, and he signals his cohort at the Center to adjust the holoboards in the area. Serena, Stone, and the other cells involved in this action will be alerted that we're inside. They'll set up a human chain along the path we've forged. Soon, an old-world bucket brigade will liberate as many B-bars as possible. A holo artist will be along to film the effort; we hope we can use the resulting footage to inspire similar low-tech, achievable revolts across the States.

"The guard situation?" I ask.

"Taken care of by the Tasmanians." Jake looks at my face and laughs. "Not dead, Somerset. Bribed. Well-bribed."

"Let's clean up," I say.

We need to pack our equipment. Jake deals with the gas. I reach for the welder gun. It turns in my sweaty hand and burns me, and I'm gasping with the pain. I drop the gun, and there's a beat and then a whoosh. And the world is on fire.

Jake drags me to the back of the building as guards burst through the front entry points. Then we're outside and running.

"The gas," Jake says. And I understand. The explosion is deafening.

CHAPTER TEN

Matthew may just be on to something because a miracle happens. No one is dead. A couple of guards suffered minor burns. My hand isn't even that bad; it just needs a small bandage. I repeat this to myself over and over as my family and I watch Matthew's office Hydra. The feed is available to officials and clerics only and for good reason; the report covers not only the fire set by "terrorist saboteurs," but the fact that after the fire was put out, citizens stormed the warehouse and determined that most of the 'Brix crates Jake and I saw there were empty. Sweet Janus. I've had enough. After checking on Monkey, I go to my room.

I get my notebook and write for a while, trying hard to exorcise the demons in my head. Only by a stroke of extraordinary luck am I not a killer. And the panic that's sure to follow the revelation that the warehouse had so little food in it? That's on me, too.

And Jake. I can barely stand to think about him, our last moments together a panicked blur. He made sure I got home safe before taking off at a run. A rap against my door interrupts my self-torment. It's my mother, who comes in and sits down on my bed. She's got fabric in her arms.

Gesturing for silence, she hands me my dun-colored sun cloak, the weightless hooded kind that every citizen in the States owns. She drapes one over her cottons and waits for me to do the same. She motions for me to follow her, and I do, through our private quarters and out the concealed back door.

We don't say all that much for a while, just the usual kind of thing: stay to the left or watch your feet. I follow my mother through the steaming city streets; they writhe violently and haphazardly with the Decemberday celebration's throngs and lack even the semblance of any underlying rhythm.

A drunken man knocks into me, and I instinctively reach for my hidden pocket. My mother does this thing then. She trips the guy, yanks me away, and moves us forward in a single move. I can't believe it.

Who is this woman?

"Looking for this?" she asks, offering me a quick glimpse of my e-tazyr. She shoves it back into her pocket.

I'm dumbfounded. But a weird part of my brain floods with relief.

"Mom!" I blubber, falling against her. We probably look like every other loopy couple out merry-making tonight.

She herds us to a dusty building in an old section of the city. My mom submits to a retscan and gets us both inside quickly. It's pre-war, this place, and the staircase looks like it was constructed with an eye for form as well as function; it has wavy carved curves that waste space. The second-story landing has three doors. My mom knocks on the middle one and does another retscan. A tall personage pulls us inside; their face looks drawn.

"Skylar, this is my daughter, Somerset. Somers, Skylar."

Skylar extends their hand. "A pleasure," they say. "Though I wish the circumstances were happier."

I'm in a carpeted room. It has dark red walls and real wood around the doors and windows. It smells like fresh laundry. I've been here before; I can feel it. A memory pulls at me: Matthew and I on the floorboards with a wheeled toy.

"I remember this place," I murmur.

My mom looks surprised. "That's amazing," she says. "You were very young."

Skylar and Mom have a whispered conversation, and then my mom leads me to a back room filled with more non-government Hydras than I've ever seen outside of Uncle Criss's house. There's somebody in front of them typing on one of the keyboards. Her chair swivels around to face us. It's Nan Wilder.

"Howdy," says Nan.

"Sweet wretched Janus," I say.

"Somerset!" yells my mom. The absurdity of her rebuke hits us both at the same time, and we actually smile.

"Kind of too late for that big talk we were going to have," I say.

"It would appear so," says my mom.

"So, you and Nan know each other," I say stupidly.

"Nan and I are cell co-heads," says my mom. "We've been at this a while."

"How long?" I ask.

"Since you were very little. I always had some secret doubts. Eventually I confirmed them. I couldn't persuade your father. He really was a true believer. A very good man, one of a long line of good people too innocent to comprehend the whole truth."

"Matthew," I say. "And lots of our friends."

My mom nods.

"How long have you been with your cell?" asks Nan. "We didn't know. We thought it was just the protests. The idea was, how hard could Taft come down on a bunch of poets?"

"For a year. With my cell. How'd you find out?" I say.

"When you began working at the Center, I guessed," says Nan. "Once I suspected, I started looking for giveaways. Eventually I was fairly sure. Your poker face needs work, Miss Whitman."

"Nan came to me, and as soon as she suggested it, I knew it was true. Somers, I'm so sorry. I should have known much earlier; I should have been paying more attention. It's been a terrible year. I tried so hard to keep your dad from revving."

My mom has tears in her eyes. So do I, and I put my arms around her.

"Your dad made me promise not to involve Matthew in any of what he called my 'theories.' He really was a pure soul who wanted the best for his family. For him, that meant certain eventual Reverie."

"I know," I say. "I tried as hard as I could to talk to him. But he was up against so many generations of training. And he wasn't capable of believing that people could be 'so wicked,' as he called it. He always told me that he believed one day, I'd see the light."

"The problem is that we have," says Nan.

Mom collects herself. "We'd like to share what Nan's dug up. It's about Monkey."

"I couldn't find anything at all," I say.

"The Hydra files were buried in a deep redaction. It took a lot of fancy footwork to find them," says Nan. "Taft's doing. Her parents were Government Center officials. Niall and Elizabeth Farrow. They stumbled upon some sensitive information. Must have been some fairly incriminating stuff; instead of re-ed, they were interrogated and, according to the records, died at some point during the process. The States arranged for Monkey's adoption. I traced the adoptive parents and sent somebody over; they're gone. The trail ends there."

"What does Monkey know?" I ask.

"Unfortunately, she witnessed her parents' arrest. Niall and Elizabeth fought back hard. Monica was very young; it's hard to say what kind of impact the experience may have had," says Nan.

I'm thinking back to the way she responded to the school pageant.

"I think she might remember some of it," I say. "What about her reaction to seeing Taft?"

"We're not sure," says my mom. "He wouldn't have been at her house that day. He has plenty of soldiers to do his dirty work."

"Unless this case was special in some way," I say.

Skylar joins us, and we all pool our information. Skylar is a tech genius, and I don't understand a lot of what they say. I wonder if they are in charge of the coded holoboards, but they don't mention it and I don't ask.

When I tell the group about Uncle Criss's holofilm, they react sort of weirdly. Like they get all self-consciously expressionless. Nobody says anything for a beat or two.

Finally, my mom speaks. "Your uncle is a good person who loves us very much. He is also a cypher. I've never been able to reconcile the man I know with his position as Head Cleric and everything that implies."

"Criss Alloy, Head Chimera," says Skylar.

I make a note to look up what that means.

The four of us talk for a long time, way beyond the curfew siren. I think that we may have to spend the night in this place, but Skylar produces a microchip for each of us to carry, something they whipped up in their spare time. It blocks the searchbirds' ability to track us. As for the patrolling soldiers, Nan's and my mom's official badges will protect us if we're stopped. I'm looking forward to getting my own when I turn eighteen; it will make my life much easier. The thought tickles something in my brain, but before I can examine it, my mind goes blurry. It's been a very long day.

When I get home, I go to my room right away. My brain feels so stuffed with revelations and new questions that it hurts; I hope to fall into a dreamless sleep.

***

When I wake up, I panic a little, remembering that Uncle Criss is sending a car for me this afternoon, and I have no idea how long I've slept. I bolt down to the kitchen to grab some food. The angle of the sun tells me it's still early in the morning, and I relax. There are no 'Brix around anymore, and so I'm forced to eat some of the delicacies my uncle gave us. A guilty pleasure, but it's just the deuce.

I find my family outside cleaning up the grounds with some volunteers. Though the Tempedral is walled off and gated, lots of Decemberday debris has landed on our property. My mom catches my eye and smiles, and something inside of me that used to ache relaxes. It's maybe gone. Monkey runs over to me and tells me that I can help with her and Matthew's job, deciding which stuff we can recycle ourselves and what must be collected.

We conduct our work quietly, a contrast to the agitation just beyond our gates. Word of the 'Brix shortage has spread quickly, and it's not difficult to hear the shouts and the alarms electrifying the city. Smoky fingers of ash funnel high into the yellow sky. Extra soldiers guard our front gates and, every now and then, Monkey eyes them uneasily. They're mostly for show, more a public relations stunt than anything else. Just like the icons and signs embedded in the façade of our Tempedral, stolen and disconnected from whatever meaning they once held. When I was fourteen, I made a study of them, using antique flatbooks for research and making a game out of finding and identifying as many of these images as I could. Learning the stories behind each began my true education. Some are logos that reference Lost Ages stuff you could buy in stores, while others were at one time considered sacred emblems of a religion or philosophy. Several more seem to be archaic stand-ins for words, like @ or #. From this study, I learned my first lesson in the tactics of the States: To mix together such diverging ideas smashes them all flat and nonsensical, leaving a void Taft and his ilk can exploit.

When Monkey says she's hungry, we decide to take a break; we invite the citizens helping us inside, but we can't persuade them. The idea of eating with us seems to embarrass them, another wretched victory for the States-imposed social order. They head to their homes. We clean up a little, rest, and then meet in the kitchen to make some food.

Matthew hears something first, and then we all do, raised voices that sound close by. My mom stays with Monkey while my brother and I go to the Great Hall, where the windows have the best view of the grounds.

"Sweet Janus!" I yell, and next to me Matthew gasps.

The front gate is down, and the yard is thick with people of all ages, chanting and stomping their feet and clapping. Some hit the front door or smash things against the building. It takes a split siren before I can make out what most of them are yelling.

"Reverie! Reverie!"

Others are screaming for our blood.

Matthew grabs my arm and pulls me into his clerical office. He's frantically looking for a Hydra connection; nothing works.

"This hasn't ever happened before," says Matthew.

We race back to Mom and Monkey and find that Nan has joined them in the kitchen. Mom looks at my face and mouths the word *cellar* before continuing her conversation. It's official. Everybody *does* know about that undocumented door.

"Taft's missing," says Nan.

"What does that mean?" asks Matthew. "And why do the crowds outside think that they can rev here? They need to go to the Kiosks!"

"They're very frightened," says Mom, pulling Monkey onto her lap. "Word has gotten out about the 'Brix shortage. And they don't know where else to go. Nan says the Kiosks are all closed; the facilitators have run."

"Uncle Criss is coming for us," I say.

Everybody stares at me.

"Yesterday he told me he'd send a car for me, but not to get in if anybody but McInnes was driving."

"A lot has happened since then," says Nan.

She doesn't know the half of it. My head is spinning.

"Listen," Nan says. "There's something you should know. Taft knew about the action at the warehouse." I look at my mom, then Matthew.

My mom nods. "Nan's caught me up. We'll discuss your promise to me—your broken promise to me—later."

"So many broken promises, so little time," I say, and she actually laughs.

"What are you talking about?" says Matthew. "What is *everybody* talking about!"

Nan continues. "The only reason you weren't all picked up is because of the fire; it threw everything off. Taft must have left his office in a hurry. The details of the sting were on his Hydra. From what I read, I think you must have an infiltrator on your team."

An infil*traitor*, I think, and I go dead cold.

CHAPTER ELEVEN

When McInnes arrives, he's not alone, and he's not in a car. Uncle Criss is with him, and they are on foot. They got here via Uncle Criss's fancy helicopter, currently located on the roof. I can't take it all in; everything is moving too fast and in a direction I can't fathom.

Uncle Criss tells my family to grab what we can in a split siren and to come with him back to his place. Matthew is as rattled as I've ever seen him, and he grabs Monkey's hand and takes her upstairs to get ready. Monkey seems okay. I'm beginning to believe that this girl has a special gift for a kind of radical acceptance; it's maybe her superpower. I'm going to follow her and Matthew, but then my uncle turns to Nan, and I hesitate. My mom, too.

"Ms. Wilder?" he says evenly.

"Yes," she says.

He waits. Nan looks confused, then pulls her official badge out of her pocket and flashes it toward him. And it hits me. The movement reminds me of what Jake did to subdue Enormous Dude at The Fallows games.

I can't see the badge's projected holo image it from my angle, but he acknowledges it with an almost imperceptible shake of his head.

"I know exactly who you are," says Uncle Criss.

Mom intervenes. "She's with us," she says firmly.

My uncle nods.

The sounds of the mob outside are louder now. Whatever is happening is escalating. The smashing sounds are louder, and the smell of smoke is strong.

"I have an idea," I say. "Everyone should get into the helicopter. I'm going to delay the citizens out front and then join you."

"What are you going to do?" asks my mom.

"I'm going to invite them in," I say. "Go! I'll be right there."

I race to my room. I grab my notebook, my mask, and Pal and shove them into my bag. I put on my dress clerical uniform quickly over my cottons; it's important that I look as authoritative as possible. I then climb the steep staircase to the third floor, where there's a huge double-hinged Plexie that leads out onto a small decorative balcony that overlooks the front yard. When I step out onto it, it sways a bit, and I'm hoping it'll support my weight. I raise my arms in what I hope is a welcoming gesture. The crowd below me calms a bit at the sight of me, and I wait before continuing. When it's a little bit quieter, I open my notebook and read, as loudly as I can, words I wrote a long time ago. My poem seems to have been waiting for this very moment in time.

"Arise and be heard, if not blessed.

Time's fateful arrow has not been

Varied, nor dissuaded from harm.

Scorned but for few, know this. We are one.

I bid you all:

Come in, come in, and be at rest.

Come inside, come in. Be at rest."

The citizens on the ground roar and surge forward. Emboldened, they begin to climb the Tempedral walls. I duck back inside, filled with a sick regret. The blameless people storming our States-sponsored castle will find some shelter inside but not a lot more.

With a last look around the only home I've ever known, I head to the roof. I discard my clerical uniform on its rough surface, the stiff fabric forming a sail in the hot wind. It's a relief to suspect I'll never wear it again.

Matthew helps me into the States helicopter, where everyone waits, bags on their laps. McInnes sits behind the control panel, and after he presses a few buttons, we ascend into the rusty sky. My heart races, and I look over at my mom. Her jaw is set, her expression inscrutable. I jabber mindlessly, trying to keep Monkey's attention on my babble rather than on the escalating madness outside the vehicle. We are flying low enough to make out some gruesome details. Desperate people do desperate things. The thought leads me to the subject I least want to tangle with. Jake, Serena, or Stone? Has one of them betrayed us all?

Uncle Criss turns to face us from his seat next to McInnes.

"When is the last time any of you ate 'Brix?"

It's the last thing I expected. We compare notes, and no one has eaten one recently.

"Just to be clear," says my uncle. "No more Nutribrix. Agreed?" he says, looking at me.

We all assent.

"Bloody hell!" yells McInnes. The helicopter swerves violently, and we all shout, trying to steady each other, and shield Monkey, who starts to cry.

"Hold on, Monkey!" my Mom yells.

McInnes' hands are flying over the control console. He's jabbing and cursing at one button in particular. He turns to my uncle.

"We've been redirected, no override. Taft. He's got us headed somewhere west; hard to say where from what I can see. I'm sorry. Now I'm just along for the ride. Everybody, brace yourselves and keep your heads. We'll be fine."

"Sweet Janus," says my uncle softly. "There are, as far as I know, only two of these currently operable in the States. Taft has the other one. He must have synched them somehow. I had no idea."

"What does this mean?" asks my mom.

Matthew looks stricken, beyond questions now. Nan is singing a rhyme I remember from my childhood to Monkey, whose eyes are closed.

"I assume we're being dragged to whatever rabbit hole into which Taft has bolted," says Uncle Criss. I look at my mom; I know we're thinking the same thing. If Monkey got so upset seeing Taft from a distance up on stage, what will happen when she sees him now?

My mom whispers our concerns to my uncle and Nan. I pull my Plexie wolf mask out of my satchel. Uncle Criss almost grins when he sees it. He knows exactly what it is. I'll think about that one later.

"You ever get tired of being a monkey that can hold on tight?" I ask her. "Let's play a game. How about if for a little while, you're not Monkey but Wolf? A wolf is loyal to her pack, that's all of us. And a wolf is strong and brave and fierce. Do you know what a wolf sounds like?"

Monkey's eyes half open, and she does a little grrrr sound.

I show her the mask, and she reaches for it. I help her fit it over her face, and Sweet Janus, it fits her perfectly; she can breathe fine, but she can't see very well. Which is the point.

"What does a wolf say?"

"Grrr," she says.

"Sometimes, wolves go AAAOOOUUUUUU!" says my mom.

"AAAOOOUUUUUU!" says Monkey.

"To play the game, you keep on the mask until it's someone else's turn to wear it," I say. "That okay with you, Monkey?"

"I'm Wolf," she says. "Until the game is over."

***

The helicopter sets itself down in a run-down neighborhood I recognize. We're somewhere in the West End, a once-thriving community of relatively well-off citizens near the city center. The houses stand close together and are similarly designed, low structures with large windows and tile roofs. Now every roof is bleached a pale coffee color, and the windows are gone; warped and shredded wooden boards have been substituted for glass and Plexie.

A few hundred feet away from where we've landed, teens are in the process of destroying a Reverie holoboard. "Why wait? Why wait?" they scream. Their parents watch and hoot while drinking and yelling encouragement. People crowd the street, some chatting as though they're at a party, others putting packed boxes on carts and wagons. One enterprising family has set up a rickety stand on their front lawn selling or bartering 'Brix and small packets of crackers. It's nuts.

"Stay inside," says McInnes as he alights from the helicopter.

His feet have barely hit the ground when the door of a nearby house opens and spews out two soldiers and some big guy with a menacingly bulky silhouette; his hands play over what we are clearly meant to understand are concealed weapons of some sort. He keeps his eye on us while McInnes and the soldiers have a quick chat. McInnes returns to the 'copter and fills us in. Taft would like us all to be his guests, with an especially warm invitation specifically extended to Nan. She shudders beside me, and I put my arm around her shoulders. McInnes says Taft's message is that he means us no harm and that we'll be free to go after he and my uncle have completed some unspecified business.

"Ready to play the game, Wolf?" asks Nan.

Monkey adjusts the mask. "Ready!"

What a kid.

The soldiers escort us to a house that, from a short distance, looks as half-wrecked and shabby as its neighbors. As we get closer, I realize that its dull façade is made of a material I've never seen before. It looks woven together with strands of very thin wire. I reach out to touch it and get a shock. The exterior of this house is cool. When the soldiers usher us inside, the interior is even colder. Taft oozes toward us. He watches while one of his minions throws our bags into a corner and electronically searches us all. They confiscate my e-tazyr along with those of the older members of our party, and Taft lifts an appraising eyebrow at me before speaking.

"Welcome to my humble home. Or, as I like to call it, Plan B."

He doesn't look at all welcoming. If anything, he looks more ferociously apoplectic than usual. His face is red and puffy, and his eyes are squinty and bloodshot. He seems to be barely keeping himself in check.

"It's an advanced tech prototype, a climate-controlled safehouse, stocked with enough provisions to last quite a while. No 'Brix, of course. We've instituted a stopgap measure to postpone the inevitable. 'Brix currently sports a new ingredient. I'm quite proud of it. A long-acting form of appetite suppressant. Folks would have killed for it during the Lost Ages. It also kills the impulse to reproduce. Snuffs the libido. Of course, every medication has its unfortunate side effects." The odious man actually chuckles.

"I couldn't stop it," my uncle says to us.

Taft pretends not to have heard him. He shakes each of our hands stiffly, stopping when he reaches Monkey.

"Ah," he says. "Miss Monica. I like your wolf mask."

I think I'm going to lose it, I really do.

Uncle Criss steps in. "Grayson, I would suggest that while we have our little confab, the child be sent to rest elsewhere. Might that be possible?"

"Of course," says Taft, and does a fake little gesture, a your-wish-is-my-command kind of thing. He nods to one of the soldiers, who begins to move toward Monkey. She shrinks back up against me.

"Grayson," says Nan. "I'm thinking we have little to say to each other at this point, as for the first time, I believe we understand each other perfectly. Please allow me to escort Miss Wolf to her quarters; we have a game to continue. Right?" she says, turning to the girl. Monkey gets the thumbs up from all of us by way of hugs and whispered encouragement. She nods and takes Nan's hand.

"I shall regret the lack of your singularly revolting presence, dear Nan," Taft says, and waves Nan and Monkey away.

They leave with the soldier, who escorts them down a hallway. Here's the thing. Something on the hallway floor catches my eye, something shiny and familiar. It's a charm shaped like a teardrop, the one that my dad gave Serena for her violin case. Which she's never without.

CHAPTER TWELVE

Serena's here. Or has been here. Is she okay? What about Jake and Stone? Is Serena the spy or a victim of Taft's?

"With regards to the child," says Taft. "Very unfortunate business, the Farrows. Her parents were, at one time, confidantes of mine. Indeed, it might be said, the three of us were thick as thieves." Taft looks pleased with himself at his use of the phrase. "Which is, in fact, what we were …" Taft bows his head modestly. "While working for the greater good, of course," he adds in a mock pious voice. Everything out of this man's mouth sounds like it belongs in italics.

"What happened to them?" asks my mom.

"They succumbed to conscience."

"To conscience," repeats Matthew.

"To their version of integrity," says Taft.

"How many versions do you think there are?" says my good brother.

Taft gets up close to Matthew and snarls at him. "More than you can ever imagine."

"I'm afraid I haven't been as forthcoming as I might have been regarding Monica's history," says Uncle Criss. "I was trying to protect you all. I couldn't stop the States from eliminating her parents for high treason, but …"

"Eliminated?! The States doesn't murder people for such things! People are re-educated and come out for the better!" interjects Matthew.

My mother puts her hand on Matthew's shoulder, and speaks softly to him; I can't hear what she says. McInnes moves closer to them both.

My uncle continues. "But her new family seems to have disappeared without a trace. When you found her, Somerset, it was such an incredible thing; I thought, possibly, that it was meant to be."

"How very crypto-mystical of you, Alloy," says Taft to my uncle. "I hope this new-found spirituality has sustained you through the many services you and your clerical cadre have performed for the States. Services I believe your young nephew might find less than beneficent."

Matthew keeps his cool, and I wonder what my mom said to him.

"What happened to Monica's second family?" I ask.

"That, I assure you, I had nothing to do with," says Taft. "People vanish from the States at an alarming rate."

"Then why did Monica recognize you at the Decemberday party?"

"Ah," says the man. "She may have caught an unfortunate glimpse of me as the Farrow homestead burned to the ground. I watched."

I have no words.

Matthew yells something, and McInnes stops him from trying to reach Taft. A good thing, because Taft's soldiers look like they'd love an excuse to get busy.

Taft looks at his HydraMobile and murmurs something to one of the soldiers, who starts tapping away on his. He speaks with exaggerated calm, but his hands are fists now. "Let us apply ourselves to our business at hand. An ancient curse comes to mind. 'May you live in interesting times.' Our times are about to get exponentially more interesting, I'm afraid. A bit ahead of schedule, but what can one do? Just since we've been enjoying our little confabulation, the States have become a more desperate and violent place than ever before. Beyond our borders, the riots may be even worse. Alloy, I'll need some information. But first, some additional incentive."

He signals a soldier, who leaves and returns almost immediately. With Serena and Stone. Serena is holding some sort of fancy e-tazyr on Stone. Who's in a restraining cuff. I can't breathe. For a split siren, I can't look at Serena's face, and then I can't stand not to. Her mouth is set in a hard line and the skin over her cheekbones is stretched tight; she looks thinner and older than when I last saw her. I don't recognize the expression in her eyes. I look at Stone.

"Love hurts," says Stone, shrugging.

"The last time I saw you, you were at Serena's," I sputter.

"I went to warn her when a bud told me we might have a problem. And so."

"Serena?" I finally manage. She keeps her eyes on Stone.

"It's her family," says Stone simply. "Taft didn't give her much of a choice."

"I'm afraid I must interrupt this tender reunion," says Taft. "Alloy, I know you've got a Plan B of your own, presumably one that takes us all the way through Z. I must commend you; despite my every effort, I've been unable to discover it. But time's up."

"Your *hold* over it certainly is," says my mom, and I realize how long it's been since I heard any kind of siren.

There's a sound at the front door, and after a nod from Taft, a soldier attends to it. And then, Jake enters the room. He's in a States official's uniform, and he's wearing a badge. He's holding an e-tazyr. He doesn't so much as glance in my direction.

Jake.

"Taft, let the crew go to their homes; we can take it from here. They'll want to reach their families; parts of the city are being gassed. Anyone else here?" he says.

"Two more in the back," says Taft.

Jake finds an e-tazyr from somewhere on a belt he's wearing that carries all kinds of awful-looking stuff and gives it to Taft. He dismisses the soldiers, who take off at a run; Jake locks the door behind them.

"I'll get the other two and dismiss the corpsman. Keep your piece pointed at this one," Jake says, gesturing to me with his weapon. "She's wily, so watch her."

I'm filled with an anger so total and overwhelming that I literally go blind for a moment. Then I'm all the way back, my fury distilled into a clarity beyond anything I've ever experienced. As Jake turns to go, I can see every stitch on his field jacket, every hair on his lying head.

Matthew does this weird gurgle and would be lunging at Taft if McInnes weren't restraining him with a meaty arm across his neck and shoulders.

"Stand down," yells McInnes.

"Listen to him, Matthew," says my uncle.

Jake returns alone. "The old lady and the brat are taken care of," he says.

Taft. Nods.

"How many of them do we actually need?" says Taft, angling his head toward us.

Things happen very quickly then.

Jake throws an e-tazyr to McInnes before he shoots across the floor and tackles Taft, who's pointing his weapon at me and firing and firing. Nothing happens. Jake tazes Taft, and the man falls to the floor. Jake puts him in hand and leg restraints so quickly that his hands look like a sped-up holo-film. He kicks Taft's sabotaged weapon across the room. He springs up and looks at Serena. She throws her e-tazyr down on the floor and then collapses on top of it. Jake gently binds her hands. He goes to Stone and frees him with some metal gadget he pulls from his pocket, the same quick motion he used to flash his badge at Enormous Dude at the Fallows' casino.

Then Jake has his arms around me, and I hear my mother and Matthew gasp.

"You alright, Alloy?" says Jake.

"I'm fine, Boyo," says my uncle.

And I understand. And I slap Jake as hard as I can. I have the satisfaction of seeing him stunned.

"That's twice now," he says. "Not okay."

"Somers," says Uncle Criss, "whatever's developed between you and Jake is your own business. I assure you I have had nothing to do with it. My only instructions were to keep you safe."

Jake gives me an injured look. "I'll get Monkey and Nan."

"Do," says my uncle. "We have a lot to talk about."

Matthew has sat down, his back against the wall; he utters a sharp laugh. Stone has gone to Serena, who's sobbing.

"I'm so sorry, I'm so sorry."

I can't even think about her right now.

"Sit, everyone, please," says my uncle. "Taft, if you say a

single word in the presence of the child, you'll wish you had not." Only Uncle Criss can make that kind of statement sound gracious.

When Jake returns with Nan and Monkey, the little girl hurls herself into my arms.

"Miss Wolf," says my mom, stroking her bright hair, "let's give someone else a turn with the mask. Okay?"

"Yup," snuffles Monkey, her face up against my neck.

My mom carefully removes the mask and puts it over Taft's face. She nods to Matthew, and they roughly move Taft into a seated position on the floor. These precautions may be unnecessary; Monkey's eyelashes are drooping in a way that usually signals naptime. Very good timing on her part; I think that the conversation we're about to have will be a disturbing one.

"May I?" asks Jake, indicating the space beside me. I'm still reeling, but my brain is on overdrive, putting all the pieces together. I'm mad at him. He lied to me. Repeatedly. But he lied to help me and my family. And yet. I'm still mad. But I move over to give him more space to sit beside me.

"I don't know for sure what's happening in the other Factions, but it's end-of-days outside of here," Jake says. He nods toward Monkey; he doesn't want to scare her with details, but we all get the picture. "No Hydra viability. And the 'copter's in pieces."

"We need to do this quickly; we may not have much time," says Uncle Criss. "We'll need to get back to my lab. Please forgive me if I spare some social niceties for the sake of brevity."

Social niceties. The funny thing is, he's genuinely unaware

of how absurd this concern is given our current situation. He cannot stop being himself. I guess none of us can. I look over at Serena, a miserable heap sitting cross-legged on the floor, her bound hands in her lap. I can't help it; I begin to imagine under what circumstances would she have been willing to sell us all out. They must have been very bad.

My uncle brings me back to the present. "Somers, Matthew, please be so kind as to find the kitchen and bring us some food and water. Be quick, please; we'll wait for you before we continue our discussion."

Taft's sit-out-the-end-of-the-world kitchen is just the deuce; I don't even recognize what most of the machines in it were built to do or know what food they might process. Matthew stays quiet, but he seems okay. I start to ask him a question, but he stops me and shakes his head. We find some simple staples, and we gather as much as we can both carry. Returning to the cottage's front room, Matthew and I distribute it.

"What exactly is your job, Alloy?" says Nan.

"You've always known," says Uncle Criss. "I represent the Gift. I lead people out of their misery through the art and science of Reverie."

"Have any of you ever been at the business end of a Kiosk after a rev?" says Nan. "I have. Many times. Wrapped bodies emerge feet first on stretchers. Each stretcher is carried to the back of a States van, specially tricked out for this purpose. Each body is inserted into a metal slot. One van can carry ten. Tell me how these poor people shot ahead of the line to Heaven, Alloy."

"What about Dad?!" I blurt. "And Aunt Stella!"

"It's all very complicated" says my uncle. "Reincarnation. Let us begin with that."

"A discredited theory from the Lost Ages," says Matthew. "We all studied it in school, when we learned about the wars."

"True, for centuries, it *was* a theory rather than a reality. Saul and I always found the concept intriguing when we were kids."

"What do you mean, *was* a theory," says Mom.

"Reverie is proof," says my uncle.

"Reverie!" shouts Matthew. "You're crazy! I've been a temprat my whole life! My family and I have devoted our lives to helping people find …"

"As Nan said, what used to be called Heaven," says Uncle Criss. "Your father, of sacred memory, was a true believer. But at least two of your family have long believed that Reverie is a scheme to reduce the States' population. And your sister has reached the same conclusion."

"What the wretched hell?!" yells Matthew, looking at Mom and me.

"They are to be admired," says my uncle. "They believe exactly what the States believes it's doing."

"The government believes it's murdering its citizens?" says Stone.

"At its highest echelons, yes." My uncle looks around the room. "That's why the Tempedrals were created. To sell what was then a lethal lie." His gaze falls on Taft's masked face and lingers there before turning back to the group. "But Reverie isn't currently what they believe it to be."

Taft turns his head sharply toward my uncle's voice.

"My mission for years now has been to save as many souls as possible from Taft and his colleagues. Through Reverie, people are born anew, carried forward. Forward, but into the past."

"The past?" I say.

My uncle nods and continues. "Belief in theoretical reincarnation had persisted for centuries, but the human ingenuity to make it possible had not yet evolved. That has happened only relatively recently. Before it was discovered, Reverie was, indeed, death. The clerical caste was the brain-child of a madman: generations of families steeped in the manufactured traditions of a nightmarish false religion. A faith that was, itself, indistinguishable from the ruling fascist government. Ours. Matthew, you and your father are two of many kind and gentle people who had no reason to doubt what you'd been taught. I myself, I'm not as good. It was this dark side that allowed me to find the truth, one you and your father could never have imagined."

Matthew looks at Mom. "Let's get out of here. The man's gone out of his mind."

Uncle Criss says, "Reverie has, for many years, been not what its creators envisioned but a true gateway to rebirth. Its process and components were chance discoveries."

Sweet Janus.

"The anomaly! When you came back," I say. "After you followed Aunt Stella."

My uncle smiles at me. "You're so very bright, my dear. Yes. What you said that day was correct. No one comes back from Reverie. But I did. And what I learned in those moments was priceless. I came back, and I knew."

"You knew what?!" says my brother.

"In the Lost Ages, there were people who studied some-thing called "extended cognition." A fellow named Andy Clark proposed that the mind isn't stuck inside the confines of the human skull. Rather, it engages and integrates with external resources. It merges with the environment in all its myriad forms, including man-made devices and creations. It was a radical notion, that human consciousness can transcend its meat-and-bone prison. These ideas always fascinated me. Then, when the anomaly occurred, every-thing clicked into place. We could truly realize Reverie. I just needed time to recreate the formulaic errors I'd made. It was a delicate thing to reconstruct, and it took some time. When I succeeded, I used my influence to refresh, as it were, the Reverie protocols. Since then, every Reverie has cheated the States, transporting souls to new life. Not into the future, as was once thought. We are reincarnated, reconstituted, into the past, back into time."

"You're some sort of savior?" yells my brother. "Are you all insane? Don't you know what we've been doing all our lives?" he says, looking around.

"We're putting it together now," says my mom, gently.

"I'm all in," says Stone.

Matthew stands up, shaking now. "What are the Experi-ences then?"

"I invented them after I perfected the new Reverie proto-cols. Opportunities to convince as many as possible to accept the Gift. Accomplished by a unique chemical cock-tail, surveillance footage, and the human psyche, which always seeks to evolve. I fought the ritual brands. I lost."

My uncle begins to rise and McInnes helps him. He looks exhausted, and when he speaks again, his voice sounds very frail.

"We've all done what we can in this lifetime. Reverie is a delicate process. We need to go to my home before it's destroyed; I need the equipment there to administer the

Gift. You are all invited. Those of you who may be unde-
cided about the Gift, please come; the decision to rev or not
will, of course, be yours."

Jake speaks for the first time since our meal. "You were
right, Alloy. This place's tunnel connects to the Government
Center. It'll be our best bet."

My uncle nods and grasps McInnes's arm.

"What about Taft?" McInnes asks.

"Ah yes. Please everyone, collect your bags. Somerset,
you'll find several 'Brix in McInnes's duffle. Please unwrap
them and feed them to our deposed king. Collect your
weapon also. Taft, if you want to survive this room, eat
them very quickly."

Ugh. Not a job I would have volunteered for. But I can see
where my uncle is going with this. I know from first-hand
experience that he'll be a much more docile creature once
he eats them. If he passes out like I did, we can drag him
through the tunnels.

Under my watchful eye, Taft gobbles down the 'Brix. The
fact that I'm holding an e-tazyr on him probably helps.

"Serena?" says Stone.

Serena. My comrade-in-arms, my confidante, my best
friend. I can't look at her.

"I can never make it right, I know," she says. "Please,
please let me come with you for a while. I need to get to my
people. As soon as we get to the city center, I'll take off. If I
leave from here on foot, I'll never make it home."

"All agreed?" says Stone. "I'll take responsibility for her.
Yeah?"

We all nod, and Stone unbinds her hands.

Matthew switches places with McInnes to steady our

uncle while he walks. McInnes grabs Taft and hoists him to his feet. He increases the wingspan of his leg restraints, and Taft begins a wobbly shuffle. The 'Brix are hitting him hard, and it occurs to me that he may never have eaten any before today. Why would he?

We gently waken Monkey, and my mom tells her we're going to have what she calls a walking picnic; she's going to eat while on the move in the tunnels. I go back to the kitchen for her food, where I notice something I hadn't before in the corner of the room: Serena's beloved instrument. Fastidiously preserved and defended for countless generations of her family, this cherished beautiful thing now sits on the floor, tipped on its side, in a soon-to-be abandoned high-tech hideout. The rush of anger I feel makes me feel faint for a split siren. Serena's failed everyone. And the music she made, those transcendent breaks in our battle to survive this world, she's failed that, too.

I bring Monkey her meal. And I sling Serena's violin into its customary position, strap across her chest. As we pass through Taft's hallway, I notice Stone bend for something on the floor. He puts Serena's teardrop charm in the palm of her hand and closes her fingers around it.

CHAPTER THIRTEEN

Taft is displaying very little tolerance for the food he's been shoving down our throats for years. He's pretty woozy, so McInnes and Stone have to lift him up to the retscan that guards the door from his safehouse to the stairs that connect to the Government Center's underground tunnel system. As soon as we're all through, they let him go, and the guy slumps to the floor.

"Oops," says Stone.

"My great grandfather ate a swan once," Taft mumbles.

My uncle anticipates the unspoken question.

"We may need him. Pick him up. We must hurry."

Stone and McInnes get Taft on his feet again. I'm pleased to see that he's been sick all over his shoes.

"Skylar?" my mom asks Nan.

"We have an emergency plan that I'm sure they'll follow," says Nan. "When I find them, we'll talk and make a decision."

From the tone of her voice, I realize that Nan and Skylar are together. Which makes me think about all the ties that bind our small cadre, some tangled and some pulled so tight it hurts. I'm most worried about Matthew.

My path to this moment has been a slow burn that started with my fascination with antique flatbooks and the lost worlds they revived. For a long time, flatbooks were on the brink of being outlawed, but they eventually became so scarce that Taft and his cronies ignored them. Most clerical families consider these works fantasies. Matthew always has. His whole life, he's been effortlessly devout in a way I have both admired and feared. His faith never left any room for the kind of restlessness I seem to have been born with.

"It's a lot to think about," I say to Matthew.

"You know, I never even did an Experience," Matthew says. "I thought I didn't need to be convinced of anything. I wonder if I should have, if it would have changed anything …" His voice drifts off.

I put my arm around my brother, and he lets me for a few minutes. Then he pats my shoulder and gently disengages.

I turn to Jake and find his eyes already on mine.

"We're good, right?" he says.

"Compared to what?"

Jake smiles, and then I do, and then we really are okay again. I'm becoming as adaptable as Monkey, who is humming to herself, and sometimes hopping, down the long white, antiseptic-looking corridor. Sometimes it feels like a dreamscape, this place, like we're floating; the walls, ceiling, and floor are made of the same seamless material, and the lack of visual definition is disorienting. Sometimes the tunnel feels like a vise, a shimmering fist about to close.

"AAAOOOUUUUUU!" yells Monkey. "I'm practicing," she says. "For when it's my turn again."

Monkey's high spirits are just the deuce because the rest of us are tense, quietly gearing up for whatever comes next.

Just when it seems the shiny passageway will never end, a door becomes visible. No retscan on this side of it, and as we pass through it, I feel a little better. We're out of Taft's domain.

We emerge into the kind of small foyer that I'm familiar with through working for the Government Center. It's called The Hub, a round space with multiple doored exits leading to different tunnels. There is some debate as to the best place to head for. We decide to go to Randall. For one thing, it's located between Uncle Criss's house and Serena's place. Nan and Skylar's home is close, too. It's also one of the least important official States structures. While we figure panicked people seeking shelter have flooded it while searching for food and safety, it seems less likely that armed government types might be gathered there, too. So, we take the tunnel that leads to the school, which makes me happy. I know it's crazy, but I'm hoping to see Dr. Szabo and Mrs. Wagner and take them with us to my uncle's.

We walk. I don't know for how long; time seems utterly stopped in this monochromatic tube. Finally, a door becomes visible.

"What might your cohorts be up to, Taft?" asks Nan as we pick up our pace.

"My wife left me," wails the man.

"Shocking," says Nan. "I mean, our esteemed Center colleagues."

"I'm unwell," says Taft. "Take me home."

"We can agree on the fact that you're a very sick man," says Nan. "Focus please. Is there a protocol in place for this kind of situation?"

Taft stares at her blearily. "What situation?"

"Armageddon," I say. I like to be helpful.

"Shhh," says my mom. "Listen."

We all stop in our tracks, and no one says a thing, not even Monkey. And then we hear it. Screaming, yelling, and crashing noises. And something else. Children are chanting, a sweet undertone to the lunatic chorus surging beyond these walls. I don't understand what I'm listening to.

McInnes leaves Taft propped up against Stone and advances to the tunnel door. He opens it a crack, and then flings it wide open.

In the small room that forms a buffer between the school and the tunnels, three grade-school kids plus a woman shrink up against the wall farthest from us in a panic.

"Mrs. Collins!" I yell. I can barely tell it's her. Her usually tight hairdo is undone, her clothes torn, and her makeup smeared all over her face.

She squints and recognizes me, then starts blubbering all kinds of stuff. My mom, Nan, and Matthew go to the kids and comfort them while I hug Mrs. Collins and try to calm her down.

"Some teachers, kids, and their families came here for shelter … we thought it would be safe. Now it's not," the woman sobs. "There was a … a …"

She's moaning now. "People went crazy. I pulled as many kids as I could in here. I thought we'd get to the tunnels. But the retscans are down. We've been stuck in this room. Practicing our multiplication tables."

Sweet Janus.

"Who else is here?" I ask. "Mrs. Wagner? Dr. Szabo?"

Mrs. Collins shakes her head. "I don't know. I haven't seen them."

Something large and metallic smashes up against the

other side of the Randall door, and the kids startle then race through the door we came through.

"May I suggest we follow the example of these wise young people," says Uncle Criss. "Change of plan. Let's reverse direction and discuss our next move."

When the Randall door closes, Jake takes something from his bag, a small triangular wedge. I don't know what it was originally designed to do, but he slips it underneath the door and kicks it hard.

"Should at least slow 'em down," he says.

"Mrs. Collins," I say. "We're heading to my Uncle Alloy's house." Mrs. Collins looks dumbfounded. She stares at my uncle like he's a unicorn.

"Criss Alloy. It's a pleasure to meet you, Mrs. Collins. We are on our way to my lab, where those of us who choose to will accept The Gift of Reverie." My uncle begins to cough, and Jake gives him some water.

Mrs. Collins laughs out loud. I can imagine what she's thinking.

"I'm sure you have a lot of questions. My lovely sister-in-law, Meredith, will answer them while we travel. If you would, my dear?"

My mom nods.

My uncle looks terribly tired, and I feel a surge of fear and adrenaline. We need a new route to his house, fast.

"The Fallows," says Serena.

We all turn to her.

"There's a passageway to The Fallows somewhere down here. Taft sent me one time."

The Fallows. Why do all roads seem to lead there?

Serena says, "It's wretched weird, I know, but Taft's always had eyes and ears in the place. Recruits," she says bitterly, "like me. He thinks his best intel comes from The Fallows. Everybody wasted most of the time, gaming and talking without thinking; the cameras are always all busted up, so people spout off without worrying."

"Bloody hell," says Jake. "I practically live there, and I didn't know that. Taft? This true? There's a tunnel to The Fallows?"

Taft mumbles something from underneath my despoiled wolf mask. I can't make it out. McInnes scoops up Monkey and says, "Miss Monica. The bad man who scared you at the big party is here with us. He's wearing the wolf mask for the game, but I think the game is over now. That okay?"

Monkey nods.

"We are taking the bad man to a place where he can't hurt anybody ever again. So, don't worry. We need to take his mask off. You good with that?"

Monkey nods again.

"Don't let him scare you, Miss," McInnes says, hoisting the little girl up higher, sitting her in the crook of his elbow. "He can't hurt anyone ever again."

He nods at Stone, who ungently takes off Taft's mask. Monkey looks at the man and bites her lower lip. She hides her face against McInnes's shoulder. But she's okay.

"It's true," says Taft. "Back to The Hub." He waves his hand vaguely.

"Aren't The Fallows the most dangerous place we could head for?" asks Matthew.

"It's not that bad," I say. My family looks at me like I've sprouted wings. "And Jake and Serena have contacts there."

"Could be that the worst of its crowd have gone to the

Center to vent their dissatisfactions," says Nan. "Not a lot to loot and plunder in The Fallows."

"This guy I buy ... refreshment from. He's got a truck he keeps hidden for deliveries. We could head there and see what's up," says Stone.

"Let us proceed," says my uncle. "My house is not too far from there to walk if need be."

Jake meets my glance, and I know we're both thinking the same thing. How much longer can Uncle Criss keep going? His skin is darker than mine, but his face now looks weirdly pale, ashen with exhaustion and worry.

It seems to take twice as long to retrace our steps back to The Hub. McInnes carries Monkey, and Stone and Jake manage Taft. Matthew, Serena, and I help my uncle, supporting him in a way that keeps the older man vertical and magisterial. Mrs. Collins shepherds her kids along while my mom speaks to her in a low voice, explaining our hijacking Taft's safehouse and Uncle Criss's recent revelations. *Rev*elations.

When we finally reach The Hub, we sprawl on the gleaming floor and distribute some of the food and water we've saved from Taft's safehouse. Mrs. Collins asks the students with her to rest in a corner and pulls my mom and brother aside; I can't hear what she wants to talk about, but the discussion turns heated. When it winds down, Mrs. Collins goes to her three charges and speaks in a soft voice. She then turns to the rest of us.

"Thank you very much for your help. Meredith has explained what's going on, where you're headed, and why. The children and I won't be going with you. It's not my time," she says. "And I can't make that kind of decision for them. We're going to head to Taft's safehouse and wait there until I can locate their parents."

She doesn't really make much eye contact with anyone, and I get it. She doesn't believe my uncle. She's had fifty or so years of steady indoctrination and can't pivot. We wish her and her kids well and show them the right doorway.

"In the fullness of time," says Mrs. Collins as they leave. We wave goodbye, a gesture which seems so normal it's almost comical.

"We've got to go," I say.

"It'll be a quick trip," says Serena. "It takes a while on foot, but as the crow flies, we're pretty close to The Fallows."

"As a mole runs, you mean." I don't even know if she gets the Lost Ages reference, but it gives me some satisfaction to say this.

Before we leave, Jake gives e-tazyrs to all the grownups, including Matthew, who looks mortified.

"Stay together and keep your eyes open."

"Time is of the essence," says Uncle Criss. "Our window for Reverie is closing fast."

CHAPTER FOURTEEN

Serena's right. It's a quick trip to The Fallows, made quicker by our new expertise in collaborative travel. Here's the thing. We're all completely drenched in perspiration by the time we get to the exit. The air system has failed, the tunnels' characteristic fresh cool air replaced by the noxious stuff most of us in the States breathe every day. Nobody mentions it. Monkey looks crumpled. Uncle Criss looks even worse.

"I need to find Skylar," says Nan. "Thank you for your kind offer," she says to my uncle. "But Skylar and I have a plan in place. I wish you all well. You are fine people."

Nan goes to my mom, and they hug each other tightly. Then she embraces the rest of us quickly and is through the tunnel's exit in a flash. I hope I'm anywhere near as smart, tough, and spry as her when I'm her age.

"Let's get moving," says Mom.

She's got tears in her eyes, and I wonder what the odds are of seeing Nan and Skylar again.

"I have an idea," I say. "Monkey, I could use your help. That okay?"

"I'm all in," says the girl.

I look at Stone, and he shrugs and grins.

"Remember the day we met? How did we get through the crowds?" I ask.

"I'm Monica, but then I got a new name, Monkey. Because I can hold on."

"Let's show 'em, Monkey."

She climbs onto my back and holds on tight. I'm guessing that we have a bunch of sand-colored sun cloaks in our various bags; sure enough, when I ask, Jake and McInnes produce a bunch of the filmy items from their duffels. Standard gear. I ask my mom to drape one over Monkey and me.

"How do we look?" I say.

"Unremarkable," says Jake. "For once," he adds and winks at me.

I set Monkey back on her feet and make my proposal. We all move as a group through The Fallows in cloaks, with Monkey and Uncle Criss carried on our backs. We head for Stone's friend's place and try to secure his truck. Then on to Uncle Criss's.

"What about Taft?" says Matthew.

"We take him with us. No cloak. We put both his badge and Jake's front and center on his shirt. He's our shield and our cover; if we're bothered, we'll say that we're a rebel vigilante group delivering him to justice to pay for his crimes against States citizens."

"It's the truth, isn't it?" says Matthew.

"That's why it's a good story," I say.

"I suppose I can sacrifice a little dignity for some foot-speed," says my uncle.

"Let's go," says Serena.

"I thought you wanted to reach your family as soon as possible," I tell her. "We'll be fine."

"I just want to see you all make it to your uncle's. I can't undo what I've done, but it would make me feel better to help just a little."

A surge of spiky temper shoots through me. Like I care what will make Serena feel better. I'm not happy about her coming with us and I say so, but I'm overruled.

We each have some water and treat Taft to another 'Brix or three. I can't help but notice that McInnes more effectively force feeds than I do. More force than feed. Then we position ourselves to leave. McInnes carries Criss on his back while Matthew carries Monkey.

We flip up our hoods and file out the unmarked door to a narrow staircase. At the top is another door made of metal, our gateway to whatever wretched hell The Fallows has devolved into since my last visit.

The air outside is foul; it smells like the cookie batter Monkey made with melted 'Brix but even more stinky. She and Criss are gently put on their feet again.

"Breathe as shallowly as you can, but breathe," my mom whispers in my ear. "When you get stressed, you hold your breath."

"And when you get stressed, you attack harmless old drunks," I whisper back. "Try to restrain yourself."

The streets are packed, but no more so than usual. The only real difference I can see is that the gambling, drinking, and who knows what else that have always been a hidden part of this place are all out in the open now. As in everywhere. In the streets and alleys, on hardscrabble front lawns, on top of stalled or dead vehicles, the area is one big desperate party. A ferocious, hopeless anger has always fueled the low entertainments The Fallows is famous for, and it's been intensified. We all have our e-tazyrs hidden but at the ready. Jake and McInnes flank Taft; they maneuver him forward. He will be both battering ram and blocker. The rest of us form a thin wedge behind those three, Matthew and Monkey and Uncle Criss and McInnes in the center, my mom and I next, and Serena behind us. Stone sort of dances around us as we walk, keeping a lookout, strong-arming citizens aside when necessary, and navigating.

We're clipping along at a pretty good pace. Maybe Nan was right, and the most crazed partiers have gone to riot and plunder at the Government Center. Stone tells us to make a left at the next juncture. It's harder to change direction than to progress in a straight-ish line, but we all manage to hold steady and stay together. When we get to a dilapidated cottage made of corrugated aluminum, Stone motions us to its front entryway, a doorless gap in the metal.

"Francisco," Stone yells into this breach. "You in there?"

A wiry guy with a big, crooked smile appears and pastes himself against Stone in an embrace, then punches him in the shoulder. This Francisco uses a set of adjectives and nouns in greeting that I wish I could keep Monkey from hearing. He's wearing a stained FireSquad uniform. Not what I expected. Stone and his buddy go inside, and when Stone comes out again, he's alone. He dangles a starter on a States official fob.

"Who wants a ride on a FireSquad truck?" he asks.

It's not Monkey but Jake who hoots like a child on Decemberday. He may actually jump in the air a little too, I'm not sure.

"I had no idea," I tell him.

"I wish Betsy could be here," he grins.

I'd forgotten all about her.

"She's waiting for us at Criss's," he answers my unspoken query. Excellent. That cat is just the deuce.

"Francisco delivers 'refreshment' from a States official vehicle?" I say.

"Genius, right?" says Stone. "The station is a couple blocks away. Let's get going."

Jake knows a shortcut through an alley. I'm guessing he's run through it on occasion; we are near the casino, and I imagine it makes for a handy getaway. Today, mostly citizens in various positions on the ground or leaning against whatever solid objects they can find fill the alley. The passageway reeks of rotgut and vomit.

"I'm not really here," says Taft.

"I want to walk," says Monkey.

"Not a good idea," says McInnes. "We're close to the truck. Hold on a little longer, okay Miss Monica?"

"I can," says Monkey.

We reach the the Firesquad station a split siren later. It's unmarked. The building used to have a sign, just like it used to have doors, windows, and whole walls, also missing now. Inside, the place swarms with revelers. The truck is in pretty bad shape. Everything removable from its surface has been torn off, and lots of people sleep or have passed out on top of it. Its military-grade glass windows are unbroken, though, and no one is inside. It must still be locked. Hopefully, it'll run. We just need to be able to drive it away without starting a riot or running over anyone.

Jake tells me that he sees someone he knows playing cards in the dusty corner of the building, a big man with his back to us. Jake saunters over, and the guy turns around. Sweet wretched Janus. It's Enormous Dude. He doesn't look happy to see Jake, who has a hand on his e-tazyr. Jake talks to the guy, who eventually swivels around to look at us before resuming the conversation. Jake returns with an inscrutable expression on his face.

"My friend over there will clear the place out," he says.

"Why would he do that?" asks Matthew.

"For Serena's violin."

"Bloody hell," says Stone.

The pain I feel for Serena rocks me. I know her, and I know she'll give up her beloved instrument without a word of complaint because she's a good person who did a bad thing when she thought she had no other option. What would I have done in her situation? What would my truth be under the same circumstances?

"We need to hurry," says McInnes.

Serena unstraps her violin and takes it out of its case. She holds it in position; its worn, wooden curves caress her face and she smiles for a split siren. She closes her eyes and hands the violin and its bow to Jake and sits down hard on the greasy cement floor.

Jake hands off the violin to Enormous Dude. I reach for Monkey beside me, but she's not there. In a panic, I scan the room. She's gone.

CHAPTER FIFTEEN

"Monica!" I'm yelling and racing around the station.

I do a quick circuit of the place, looking for her among the drunken knots of partiers and peering into corners she might think would be fun to play in. By the time I finish, we're all on the same terrible page. Monkey is lost somewhere, has been taken somewhere, or worse. Me, Stone, Serena, and Jake instinctively move toward each other, and no words need to be spoken. We reconstitute our cell just like that.

"I'm coming," says my mom.

"Me too," says Matthew.

McInnes doesn't bother with conversation. He's halfway out the station door before Jake catches up with him. They speak briefly before both of them return and huddle with Uncle Criss. McInnes doesn't look happy. My uncle puts a hand on the big man's arm, not in restraint but in what looks like a rare show of emotion. McInnes nods.

Jake turns to my mom and Matthew, saying, "Your skill sets may be needed here. And we'll be more efficient as a practiced team. Really, this is the best way, the right thing to do. As soon as the garage clears out, get inside the truck, lock it, and wait. Here," he says, handing my mom something from his utility belt. "When this stick gets to here, go to Criss's even if we're not back yet. Start the Reverie protocols. We'll join you as soon as we can."

My mom stares at maybe the first timepiece she's ever seen. Jake actually got the thing to work. It's ticking.

"Take care of each other," says Jake.

He looks at Uncle Criss, who nods. Jake throws the truck starter to Matthew.

"What about him?" says McInnes, looking at Taft.

"He comes with us," I say. "Make sure his hands are secure and take off his badges for now."

Jake takes care of Taft, and we walk him outside.

The wrecked Kiosk I noticed the last time I was here stands close by, and we decide to use it as our meet spot. Stone draws a grid of the area in the dirt, and Jake, Serena, and I split up to run a quick foot pattern through the surrounding blocks. Stone stays with Taft; he's the slowest on his feet, and the most physically intimidating among us. We plan to meet back at the Kiosk with any intel and to hold off initiating any action until we can move as a team.

I cover my area quickly but thoroughly, galloping through the crowded pathways, scanning for Monkey or anything that looks unusual, listening for her voice or for anything that might be related to her. I come up empty. No sight or sound of the girl nor any citizen chatter that might be connected to her abduction. I feel a desperate catch in my heart unlike anything I've ever felt before. I have an epiphany: My love for Monkey isn't really that of a sibling. It's as close to a maternal connection as I am likely to have in this life.

I reach the casino. It's buzzing so loudly I can hear it from the street. And some part of my brain knows without a doubt that Monkey's in there. I race back to the Kiosk. Nobody has seen or heard anything promising.

"I think she's in the casino," I say. "I would have gone in and searched, but it sounds like wretched hell in there and I have nothing to trade or game with!"

"We've got nothing else to go on. Plus, I can't think of a more likely place to target," says Jake.

We take off at a run, even Stone and Taft, Stone pretty much airlifting the guy. Taft himself seems to be doing okay considering how many 'Brix he's eaten lately.

The casino entrance is jammed and blocked by people drinking and throwing dice. Serena sees someone she knows who's watching the game and betting on its outcome. She weaves expertly through the crowd and talks to this woman. I don't know what she says, but it does the trick; an instant later, the woman and her friends shout, push, and generally raise bloody hell in their efforts to help us. We all squeeze through the jagged path they open and go down the casino's narrow cement staircase.

The inside is as I remember it but worse, much worse. It's more densely packed, smellier, and more screamy, way more screamy. Then, sweet Janus, I see Monkey. She's almost directly below us on the slope that formed the original pool's bottom. I maneuver frantically to get closer; she spots me and starts waving and yelling my name. She's crying, and I'm furious and so, so relieved. She's being held tightly by the arm in between what looks like a couple, a man and a woman with similar tattoos. The man is crouched over, playing a card game in a large circle.

I shout her name as loudly as I can, and the others fall in right behind me as I start bashing my way toward her; they catch up, and we move forward in a wedge, our e-tazyrs ready. Maybe the one thing the States does well is regulate its weapons. If it were easier for average citizens to obtain e-tazyrs, there'd be no need for Reverie.

A teen boy lunges toward me. Jake uses the guy's own heft and momentum to send him sprawling in another direction. The kid lands on a bunch of folks who aren't happy about it, and they all start to brawl. As we move closer to Monkey and the circle of gamblers, it gets harder and harder to move. The cement below our feet is slippery, and people are moving so erratically it's hard to avoid them. I'm aware of painful jabs and knocks, but it's like it's happening to someone else. Nothing matters but Monkey.

Finally, we reach the couple holding her.

"I knew you'd find me!" she says.

Monkey's hair is wet with perspiration and grime. She looks like she's been dragged through sand and muck and tear tracks mottle her dusty cheeks.

Jake puts his hand on the woman's shoulder.

"Ho, my friend. The little girl belongs to us."

"No, she don't," says the woman. "Conrad found her outside. Alone. We never could have kids, so now we have her."

"I don't know what Conrad told you," I say, "but this child's name is Monica Whitman and she was with me and the rest of our family when she was stolen."

"You sayn' he's a liar?" yells the woman.

Her partner turns around now. "Shut the wretched hell up! I'm working here!"

Jake speaks up. "Do you know who this is?" he says, pointing to Taft. "Take a look, friends." He reattaches the States official badges to the front of Taft's shirt.

The man and woman's eyes are glazed over, unfocused; they seem to be unable to process what they're seeing. Stone gives them a little help.

"Who is the most hated man in the States? Who's responsible for every evil day of bloody hell?" he booms.

Now the other circle players pay attention.

"Who feeds us wretched 'Brix?" Serena cries.

"Bloody Taft!" someone yells. "Taft! Taft! Taft!" people start chanting.

"Ladies and gentlemen, personages and others, I give you Grayson Taft!" I yell. "He is now under the care and feeding of … Conrad!" In a lower voice, I add, "We're armed. Give us our little girl, and we'll give you Taft. He should be worth a lot."

Conrad and his partner look at each other, and the woman nods and releases Monkey. She runs into my arms.

"You know what to do," I whisper, and she climbs up onto my back.

"Taft stays here, with you!" yells Jake, and the crowd roars. "We leave now! We'll bring you more!"

"More?" I say as we move out, as quickly as we can.

"Hey, I'm improvising. Giving everyone a reason to let us go without a fuss," Jake says.

Monkey tightens her grip on my neck, her fingernails digging into my skin like fiery pinpoints.

"It's okay, Monkey," I say. "Easy peasey from now on."

She holds on even tighter in response.

We're almost at the exit when I do it. I can't help myself. I turn around and look back at Taft. What I see is a lump on the cement. A group of citizens has converged over his body, their legs kicking at him. For a split siren, I think I catch a glimmer of one of Taft's badges. I feel nothing; no shame or remorse. Or satisfaction.

Outside the casino, a surprise awaits us. With Matthew behind the wheel, the FireSquad truck pulls up to the entrance. The doors swing open, and he yells for us to hurry.

"You were supposed to go to Uncle Criss's!" I say.

"Yeah," says Matthew. "I'm a bad rebel."

I look over at my uncle. He seems a bit better, and he actually gives me a thumbs up. Which makes me grin. I've never seen him do anything so unrefined.

"How'd you know where we were?" I ask Matthew.

"The streets are buzzing with the news that Taft's here. Word travels fast. Let's see if we can, too."

He switches on the firehorns, and we skid out of there; citizens are used to dodging these trucks and for the most part, they get out of our way.

"I need to get home," says Serena.

"We're going right past your neighborhood," says Matthew. "We'll drop you off."

"Serena," I start.

"Please don't," she says.

"I was just going to thank you for all your help," I say. "Please forgive yourself. *I* forgive you." It's only as I say it that I realize it's true.

"Me too," says Stone. "And I'm the one you were ready to e-tazyr into the Lost Ages."

Serena holds a hand up to silence us, then puts it over her eyes and slumps forward. We are all quiet for a bit. My mom's arm rests around me and I lean into it, letting myself relax into the exhaustion.

The streets teem with people on foot, in carts, and even some in vehicles. Whole families are traveling with odd pieces of luggage and furniture, and one group has a cage of chickens with them. Real chickens! We all stare at them from the truck's windows as we pass.

We turn onto a side street that looks almost familiar to me. Like I should know it, but I don't. The horror sets in slowly. When we pull up in front of Serena's place, no one says a word. It's not a house any longer but a pile of corrugated metal and rubble. One of its broken walls stands propped up against a neighboring fence, and you can read the faded slogan on it: Farm-to-Table Freshness!

Serena cries out and leaps from the truck. She runs toward the ruins but has to stop when she gets to where the front door used to be; there's literally no place to go. Stone runs right behind her and catches her as she stumbles backward. He scoops her up and carries her to the FireSquad truck. McInnes and my mom ease her into a seat, and Stone follows.

"Go!" says Stone.

Matthew peels out of there fast. I'm wondering if we're all sharing the same thought. What if Uncle Criss's house is in the same condition as Serena's?

CHAPTER SIXTEEN

Uncle Criss's retreat still stands but is surrounded. If it was originally designed to mimic a Lost Ages fairytale castle, as I've always suspected, it's been properly stormed. Its gates are down, and there are little fires all over the front yard. The scene is surreal, but horribly similar to everywhere else we've been on our way here. Citizens lurch about, smoking, drinking, gambling, and fighting. People are all over the house's uneven stone surface, literally climbing the walls and bashing in windows where they can find real glass. It's an end-of-the-world free-for-all.

Matthew doesn't stop. He zooms by the house at top speed before turning down an alley a few blocks away and idling the engine.

"The right decision, my boy," says my uncle. "I'll give you directions."

"Directions to?" asks Stone.

It hits me before my uncle has a chance to answer. Of course. I make a mental note to ask him if all Tempedrals have these secret passageways, or just our family's.

"Ingress and egress. History would indicate they often ultimately determine the winners and losers of a siege. I feel very badly for the poor souls I couldn't save, but I've worked very hard to free as many as I could. Let us try to survive ourselves, now."

He gives Matthew some simple directions; it sounds like we will circle around to the front door. But then, he asks Matthew to stop in front of a run-down cottage mostly hidden by discarded building materials. I figure the place is roughly parallel to the back of Uncle Criss's property.

Matthew stops the truck, and we wait for McInnes to do a quick inspection before he lets us inside. The cottage remains in fairly decent shape, modestly furnished and mostly intact. Some pictures that hang on the walls look interesting, paintings made of tiny dots that seem to emit light and dance before my eyes.

We all seem pretty okay, considering. Except for Serena. She looks dazed, and if Stone wasn't guiding her, I'm not sure she wouldn't just let herself slip to the ground. We each get some water and divide the last of the remaining food. I'm happy to see that Monkey's appetite hasn't been dampened by her recent ordeal. This girl is a survivor.

"As I did with your Tempedral," Uncle Criss says, nodding at my family, "I built something extra into my retreat. I designed both homes with an emergency entrance and exit. This house has a passageway that leads to my lab. I suggest we make haste. Our path is going to be very warm, roughly the outside air temperature but with less oxygen. You'll be more comfortable if you remove non-essential clothing. No need to worry about the sun. If all goes well, you've been exposed to this sun for the last time."

Unsaid: If things don't go well, it won't matter what we are wearing.

Monkey has fallen asleep. My mom and I remove her sun cloak, and then our own. We all strip down to the essentials. My mom and I decide to take off our shirts like the guys and travel in our bralettes; it feels weird but comfortable. I go over to where Stone is helping a listless Serena out of her cloak.

"I'm so sorry," I say. "I know how you feel. I didn't before my dad revved, but I do now."

"I tried so hard to keep us together," Serena begins, but I interrupt her. I've just had a terrible thought.

"Serena, do you think that the disk we played at your house had anything to do with what happened? So many people could have overheard it! What if somebody said something to the wrong person?"

Then my arms wrap around her and hers around me, and we're both rocking. With grief, with the unfairness of it all, with the burden of our failures.

McInnes starts barking orders at us. It's time to go.

***

The passageway is narrow, low-ceilinged, and unevenly paved with thick square rocks I've only seen in flatbooks before. Uncle Criss was right to warn us. I remember an antique word, claustrophobia; I guess no one uses it anymore because it's our steady state reality. Our steady *States* reality. But this tunnel makes me uneasy in a way I'm not used to. It feels like it could cave in at any moment. And as Uncle Criss promised, it's very hot. We all start to discard any more clothing we can and still stay decently covered, but I can imagine that concern eventually fading; it depends on how long it takes us to reach the lab.

One by one, except for McInnes, we drop our satchels. I feel the lighter for it, but also crazy sad as I part from the journal I've kept for so many years. Maybe someone will find it one day and come to know me, my family, and the way we lived. How we tried to make changes to the way we lived.

My mom looks unwell. Matthew and I walk on either side of her, each of us cradling an elbow and forearm. Stone has Uncle Criss on his back now; despite the ignominy of my uncle's situation, he has a peaceful expression on his face. It makes me feel better, like this might all actually end up being okay. Jake marches protectively ahead of us, his e-tazyr in hand. Serena seems to have gotten a second wind and does the same thing just behind us.

McInnes calls a halt. He takes water out of his duffel and gives everyone a small amount. Then he takes off his undershirt and rips it into strips. He soaks each strip in water and instructs us to tie them around our foreheads. Except for Monkey. McInnes pours the last drops of our supply over Monkey's overheated small head and then ties on a wet headband for her.

"Monster's gotcha," growls the big man. "Just a little bit further." He gently picks her up and carries her.

We walk. This tunnel feels endless, a place where time is measured in shallow breaths and hard-won inches forward. Jake holds his hand up and we stop as he examines something on the ground. He turns around and catches my eye; he looks like he's going to cry, and I hurry toward him. It's Betsy. She's dead. Her fur is stiff and dusty. Then I realize it's not dust on her body but some white grainy substance that's giving off a weird smell.

"Don't touch her," says Jake. "She must have gotten into something in the lab. Poor Betsy."

"Jake! I'm so sorry." I press my body up against his, my arms around his chest. It feels like home.

"She was a good friend. Very nonjudgmental. And lucky. She had a fine life, I think."

"I know she did," I say. "How is she even in here, though?"

"I don't know," says Jake. "She shouldn't have been able to leave your uncle's living quarters."

We go back to the others and catch them up and, using language Monkey is unlikely to understand, caution them against touching the animal. McInnes makes sure Monkey doesn't see Betsy, but everyone else takes a long, wondering look as we pass her.

A doorway frame appears around a bend. Finally. The sight of it makes us all pick up our pace. Once again, though, Jake holds up his hand. We wait while Jake looks around. His face is set and grim when he comes back to us.

"The door's open," says Jake. "Just a crack. I don't hear anything on the other side."

My uncle frowns, then shrugs.

"There's no time to fret about it. We need to keep going, we have no choice," he says.

A split siren or two later, we're all in my uncle's lab. It looks nearly exactly as I imagined it would, all silvery and shimmering and mysterious.

"Fortune has favored us," says my uncle. "The lab is intact, and I'm well enough to do the procedure. McInnes, be so kind as to lock the doors."

I feel a rush of air, and I'm shoved against a hard surface by a figure in some kind of dark clothing. The floor leaps up to meet me. I move my legs, but they stay still. The pain in my head is a live thing clawing at the inside of my skull. I can't see; everything is liquid and dark.

I hear shouts and groans. Somebody shakes me. It's Monkey, her tiny hands on my shoulder. I embrace her and turn my back to the room, sculpting a concave space for her between me and the wall.

Screaming. The words Reverie, mandate, and treason. Two voices I don't recognize. Something heavy crashes to the floor. Scuffling. It's all happening so fast.

Serena cries out Stone's name over and over. McInnes says he's gone, he's gone.

Jake, by my side. His lips on mine. "We're going to Rev now," he says. All except for Matthew. He's staying to help those left behind. He's made up his mind.

Matthew's cheek against mine. Then something else, something smooth and familiar. "I picked up your note-book after you left it," he whispers. "I'll read it. And I'll pass it on."

Monkey's soft braids under my chin. Her quick breaths against my neck.

Serena presses something into my hand. Her teardrop violin case charm.

My uncle's voice, calm and authoritative. "Lift," he says. "She needs to go now."

I'm in a bed. This one is narrower than my bed at home; I can feel its metallic sides with the palms of my hands only a half inch away from my hips. Its sheets are cool and soft. I want my mom. Like magic, I feel her strong arms around my shoulders and her soft hands against my forehead, smoothing back my hair. She whispers in my ear. She loves me. "We'll be with each other again," she says.

In the fullness of time, I think.

ACKNOWLEDGEMENTS

Thanks to Gary Rubin and Tom Tolley, co-conspirators extraordinaire. Jessica Bell, Amie McCracken, Melissa Slayton, Gloria Russell, Elizabeth Rose, Andrea Caswell, Bonita LeFlore, Laurie Mendoza, Linda Sanchez, Paula E. Breger, Michael Finnegan, Tori Gifford, and Kim DiCamillo provided me with invaluable feedback. Thank you so much! As for my husband Charlie, and daughters Alison and Liza, loves of my life, "Even you know it."

VINE LEAVES PRESS

Enjoyed this book?
Go to *vineleavespress.com* to find more.